A TREASURY OF XXth CENTURY MURDER

Lovers' Lane

ISBN: 978-1-56163-628-0
Library of Congress Control Number: 2012937346
© 2012 Rick Geary
Printed in China

1st printing June 2012

Comicslit is an imprint
and trademark of

NANTIER • BEALL • MINOUSTCHINE
Publishing inc.
new york

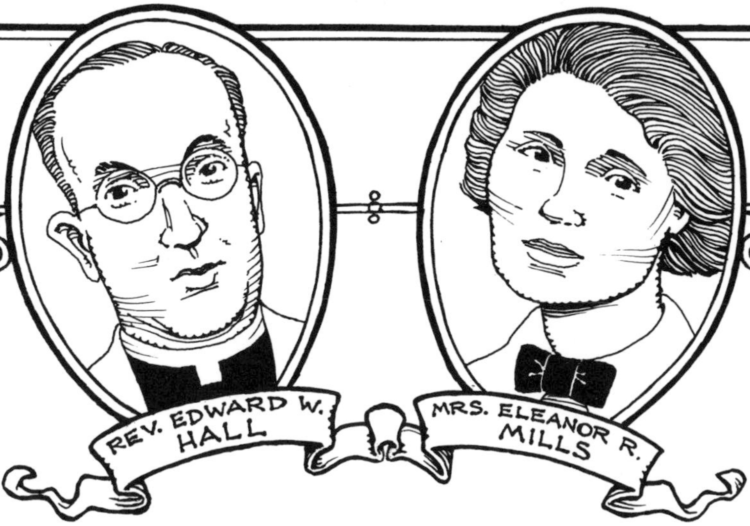
REV. EDWARD W. HALL
MRS. ELEANOR R. MILLS

LOVERS' LANE

THE HALL-MILLS MYSTERY

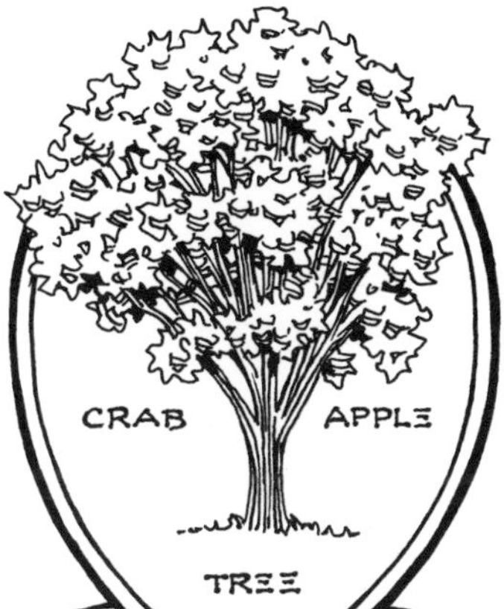
CRAB APPLE
TREE

WRITTEN & ILLUSTRATED BY
RICK GEARY

LOVERS' LANE
The Hall-Mills Mystery

BIBLIOGRAPHY

Crimes of Passion, no author credited. (London, Verdict Press, 1975)

Kunstler, William, *The Hall-Mills Murder Case.* (New Brunswick NJ, Rutgers University Press, 1980)

Thurber, James, "A Sort of Genius," reprinted in *The Mammoth Book of Unsolved Crimes*, Roger Wilkes, ed. (New York, Carroll & Graf, 1999)

Tomlinson, Gerald, *Fatal Tryst: Who Killed the Minister and the Choir Singer?* (Lake Hopatcong NJ, Home Run Press, 1999)

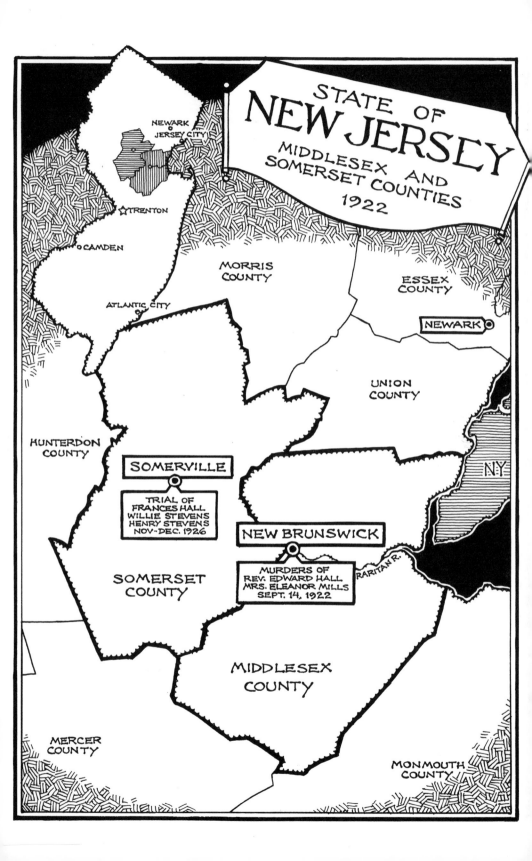

STATE OF
NEW JERSEY
MIDDLESEX AND
SOMERSET COUNTIES
1922

NEWARK
JERSEY CITY

☆TRENTON

CAMDEN

MORRIS
COUNTY

ESSEX
COUNTY

NEWARK

ATLANTIC CITY

UNION
COUNTY

HUNTERDON
COUNTY

NY

SOMERVILLE

TRIAL OF
FRANCES HALL
WILLIE STEVENS
HENRY STEVENS
NOV-DEC. 1926

NEW BRUNSWICK

MURDERS OF
REV. EDWARD HALL
MRS. ELEANOR MILLS
SEPT. 14, 1922

RARITAN R.

SOMERSET
COUNTY

MIDDLESEX
COUNTY

MERCER
COUNTY

MONMOUTH
COUNTY

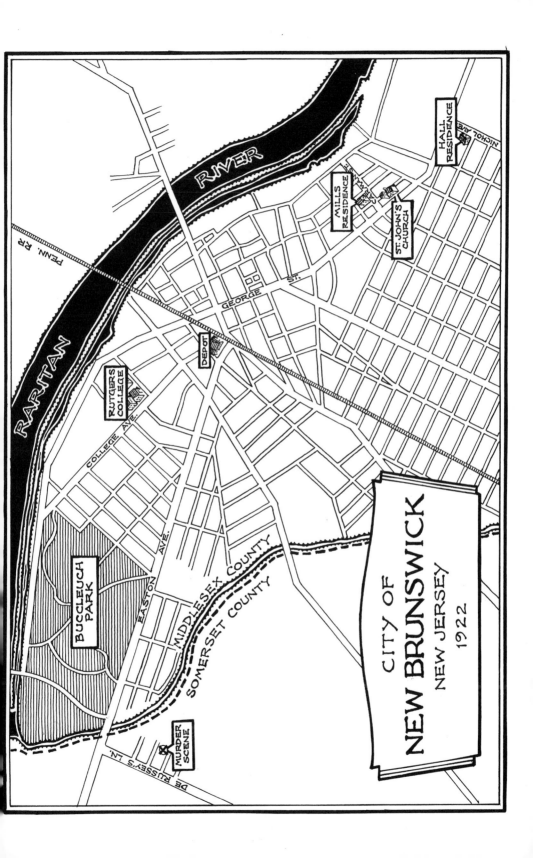

RIVER

RARITAN

PENN. R.R.

HALL RESIDENCE

NICHOL AVE.

MILLS RESIDENCE

ST. JOHN'S CHURCH

GEORGE ST.

DEPOT

RUTGERS COLLEGE

COLLEGE AVE.

BUCCLEUCH PARK

EASTON AVE.

MIDDLESEX COUNTY

SOMERSET COUNTY

MURDER SCENE

DE RUSSEY'S LN.

CITY OF
NEW BRUNSWICK
NEW JERSEY
1922

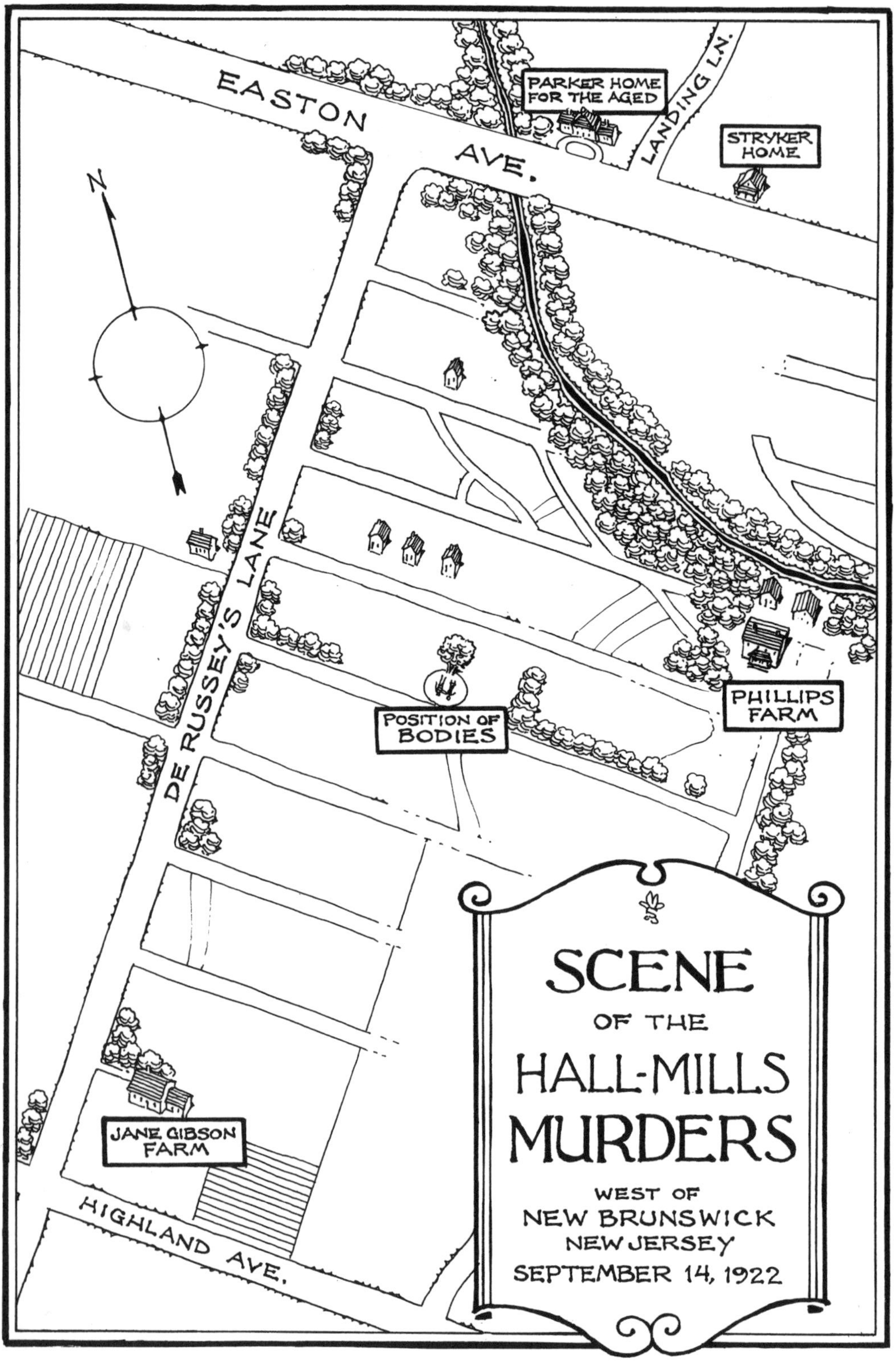
EASTON AVE.
PARKER HOME FOR THE AGED
LANDING LN.
STRYKER HOME
N
DE RUSSEY'S LANE
POSITION OF BODIES
PHILLIPS FARM
JANE GIBSON FARM
HIGHLAND AVE.
SCENE
OF THE
HALL-MILLS
MURDERS
WEST OF
NEW BRUNSWICK
NEW JERSEY
SEPTEMBER 14, 1922

PART I

UNDER THE
CRABAPPLE TREE

1922
NEW BRUNSWICK, NEW JERSEY, IS A VIBRANT AND
PROSPEROUS TOWN ON THE BANKS OF THE RARITAN RIVER.

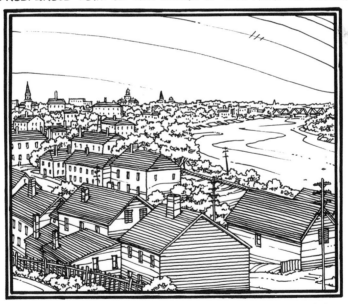

WITH A POPULATION OF ABOUT 33,000, IT MIGHT BE
CALLED THE TYPICAL AMERICAN COMMUNITY.

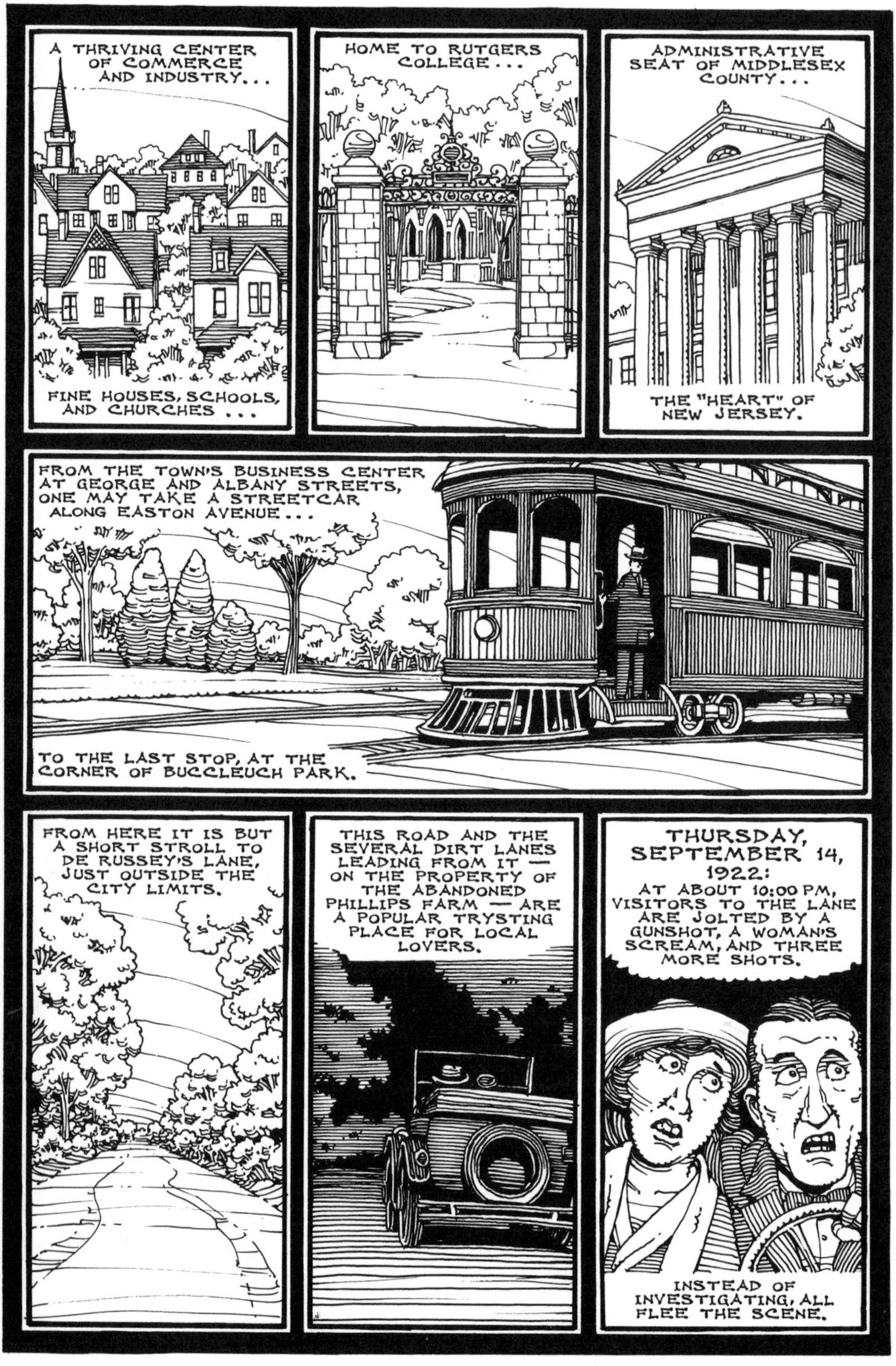
A THRIVING CENTER OF COMMERCE AND INDUSTRY...
FINE HOUSES, SCHOOLS, AND CHURCHES ...
HOME TO RUTGERS COLLEGE...
ADMINISTRATIVE SEAT OF MIDDLESEX COUNTY...
THE "HEART" OF NEW JERSEY.
FROM THE TOWN'S BUSINESS CENTER AT GEORGE AND ALBANY STREETS, ONE MAY TAKE A STREETCAR ALONG EASTON AVENUE...
TO THE LAST STOP, AT THE CORNER OF BUCCLEUCH PARK.
FROM HERE IT IS BUT A SHORT STROLL TO DE RUSSEY'S LANE, JUST OUTSIDE THE CITY LIMITS.
THIS ROAD AND THE SEVERAL DIRT LANES LEADING FROM IT — ON THE PROPERTY OF THE ABANDONED PHILLIPS FARM — ARE A POPULAR TRYSTING PLACE FOR LOCAL LOVERS.
THURSDAY, SEPTEMBER 14, 1922:
AT ABOUT 10:00 PM, VISITORS TO THE LANE ARE JOLTED BY A GUNSHOT, A WOMAN'S SCREAM, AND THREE MORE SHOTS.
INSTEAD OF INVESTIGATING, ALL FLEE THE SCENE.

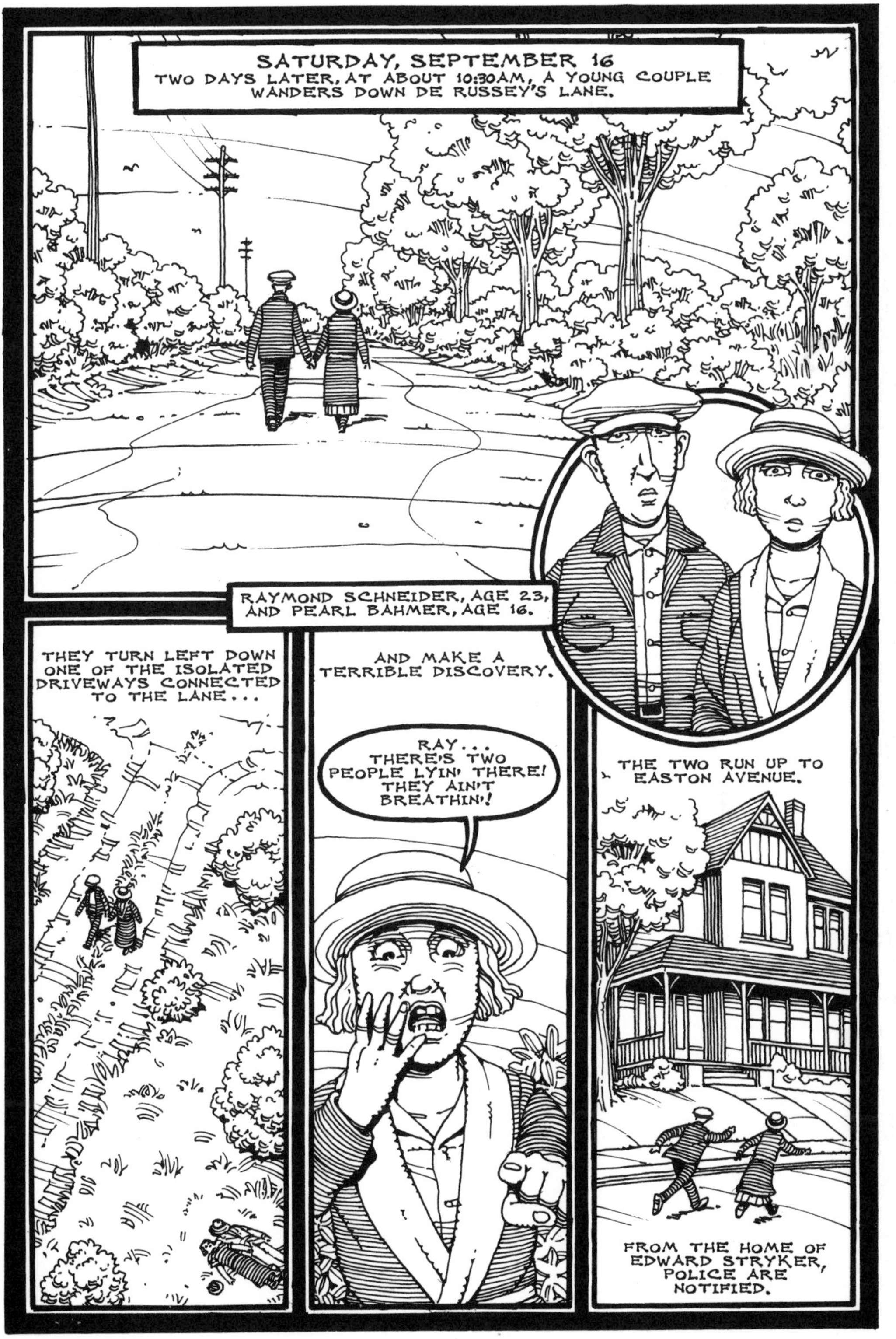
SATURDAY, SEPTEMBER 16
TWO DAYS LATER, AT ABOUT 10:30AM, A YOUNG COUPLE WANDERS DOWN DE RUSSEY'S LANE.
RAYMOND SCHNEIDER, AGE 23, AND PEARL BAHMER, AGE 16.
THEY TURN LEFT DOWN ONE OF THE ISOLATED DRIVEWAYS CONNECTED TO THE LANE...
AND MAKE A TERRIBLE DISCOVERY.
RAY... THERE'S TWO PEOPLE LYIN' THERE! THEY AIN'T BREATHIN'!
THE TWO RUN UP TO EASTON AVENUE.
FROM THE HOME OF EDWARD STRYKER, POLICE ARE NOTIFIED.

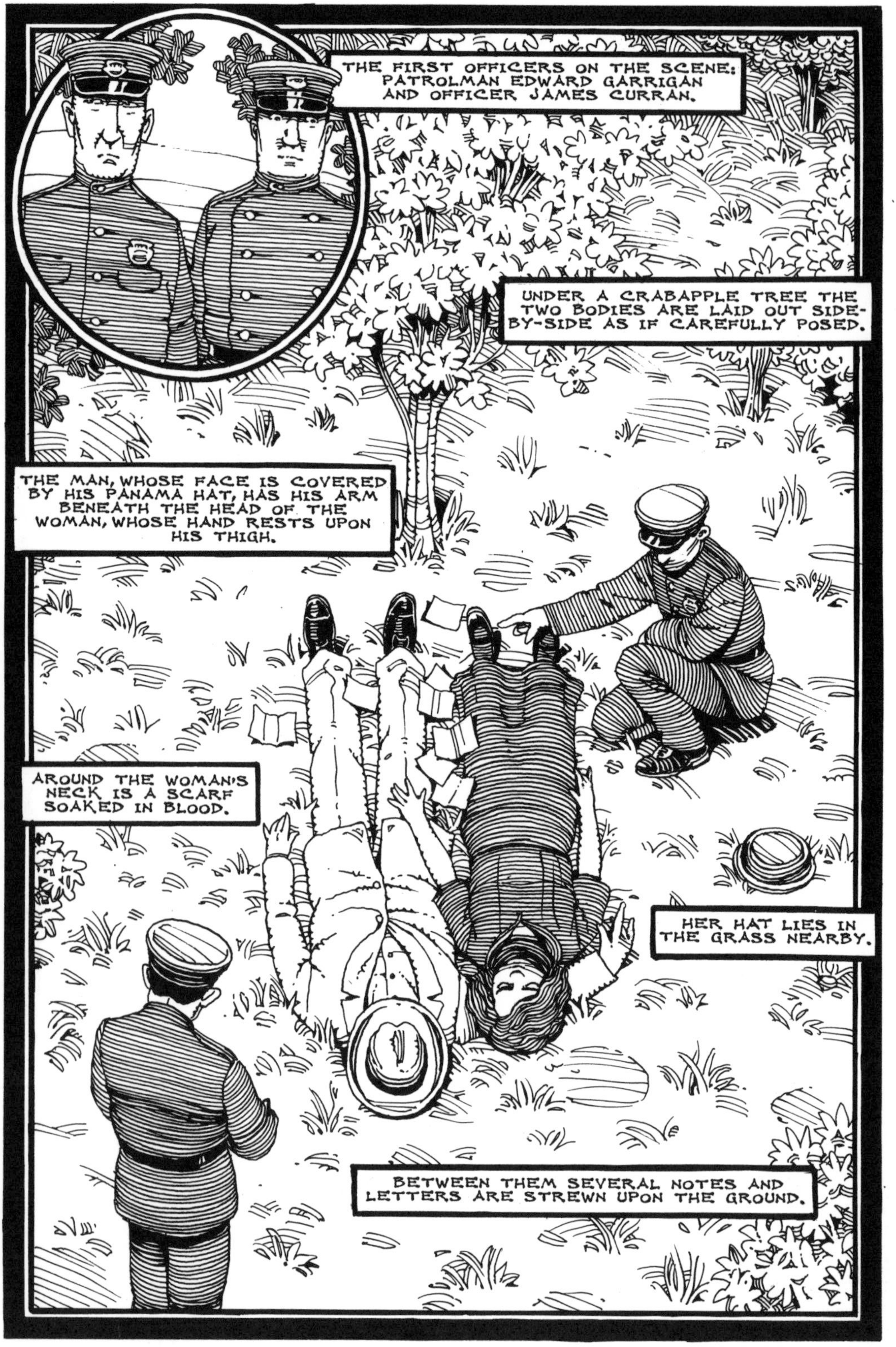
THE FIRST OFFICERS ON THE SCENE: PATROLMAN EDWARD GARRIGAN AND OFFICER JAMES CURRAN.
UNDER A CRABAPPLE TREE THE TWO BODIES ARE LAID OUT SIDE-BY-SIDE AS IF CAREFULLY POSED.
THE MAN, WHOSE FACE IS COVERED BY HIS PANAMA HAT, HAS HIS ARM BENEATH THE HEAD OF THE WOMAN, WHOSE HAND RESTS UPON HIS THIGH.
AROUND THE WOMAN'S NECK IS A SCARF SOAKED IN BLOOD.
HER HAT LIES IN THE GRASS NEARBY.
BETWEEN THEM SEVERAL NOTES AND LETTERS ARE STREWN UPON THE GROUND.

PROPPED AGAINST THE MAN'S SHOE IS A CALLING CARD: THAT OF THE REVEREND EDWARD W. HALL OF THE CHURCH OF ST. JOHN THE EVANGELIST IN NEW BRUNSWICK.

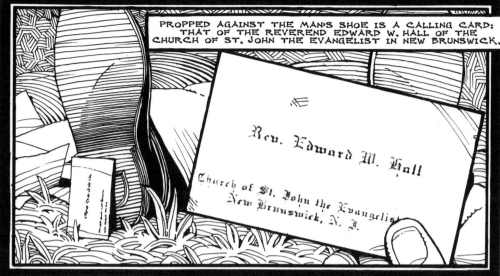

Rev. Edward W. Hall

Church of St. John the Evangelist
New Brunswick, N. J.

A CARD CASE FOUND NEARBY CONTAINS A DRIVER'S LICENSE, AUTO REGISTRATION, MEMBERSHIPS IN THE YMCA AND MASONS — ALL BELONGING TO THE SAME REVEREND.

STATE OF NEW JERSEY

Y.M.C.A.

OFFICER CURRAN LEAVES TO CALL HEADQUARTERS AND SUMMON MORE OFFICERS.

GARRIGAN IS LEFT IN CHARGE OF THE SCENE.

AT THIS POINT THE FIRST REPORTER ARRIVES: ALBERT CARDINAL OF THE NEW BRUNSWICK DAILY HOME NEWS.

HE IS ALLOWED TO APPROACH THE BODIES AND EXAMINE THE CALLING CARD.

CURRAN RETURNS WITH A PASSING MOTORIST, DR. LEON LOBLEIN, A LOCAL VETERINARIAN...

WHO IDENTIFIES THE MAN'S BODY AS THAT OF REVEREND HALL.

SINCE THE BODIES LIE JUST OVER THE LINE INTO SOMERSET COUNTY, OFFICIALS FROM SOMERVILLE ARE CALLED IN:

SHERIFF BOGART F. CONKLING, DETECTIVE GEORGE TOTTEN, AND COUNTY PHYSICIAN WILLIAM H. LONG.

EVEN THESE MEN FAIL TO SECURE THE AREA FROM THE CURIOUS CITIZENS WHO ARE BEGINNING TO ARRIVE IN NUMBERS.

CONKLING SCRUTINIZES THE LETTERS SCATTERED BETWEEN THE BODIES.

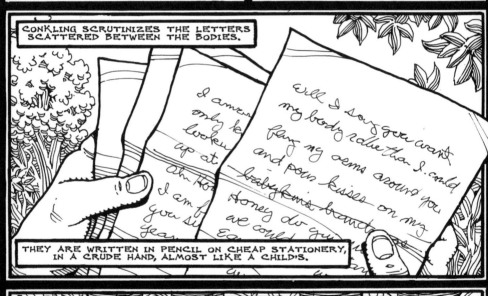

THEY ARE WRITTEN IN PENCIL ON CHEAP STATIONERY, IN A CRUDE HAND, ALMOST LIKE A CHILD'S.

EDWIN R. CARPENDER, A COUSIN OF THE REVEREND'S WIFE, ARRIVES TO MAKE A FORMAL IDENTIFICATION OF THE MAN'S BODY.

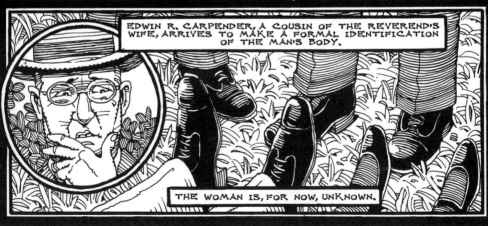

THE WOMAN IS, FOR NOW, UNKNOWN.

AFTER A CURSORY EXAMINATION, DR. LONG DECLARES THAT, IN VIEW OF THE ADVANCED STATE OF DECOMPOSITION, THE VICTIMS HAVE BEEN DEAD FOR ABOUT 36 HOURS.

THIS PLACES THE MURDERS AT ABOUT THE TIME THAT SHOTS WERE HEARD IN THE LANE ON THURSDAY NIGHT.

COULD THE BODIES HAVE LAIN HERE FOR SO LONG WITHOUT BEING NOTICED?

OR WERE THE VICTIMS KILLED ELSEWHERE AND SIMPLY DUMPED HERE?

AT ABOUT 2 PM, THE SOMERSET COUNTY UNDERTAKER, SAMUEL SUTPHEN, ARRIVES.

THE REMAINS ARE REMOVED TO HIS FUNERAL HOME IN SOMERVILLE.

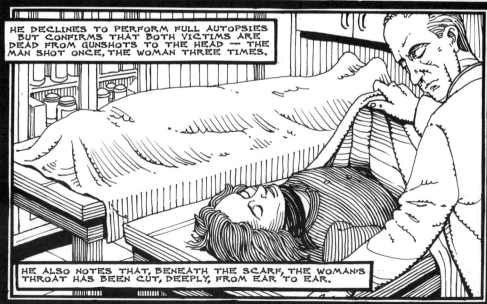

HE DECLINES TO PERFORM FULL AUTOPSIES BUT CONFIRMS THAT BOTH VICTIMS ARE DEAD FROM GUNSHOTS TO THE HEAD — THE MAN SHOT ONCE, THE WOMAN THREE TIMES.

HE ALSO NOTES THAT, BENEATH THE SCARF, THE WOMAN'S THROAT HAS BEEN CUT, DEEPLY, FROM EAR TO EAR.

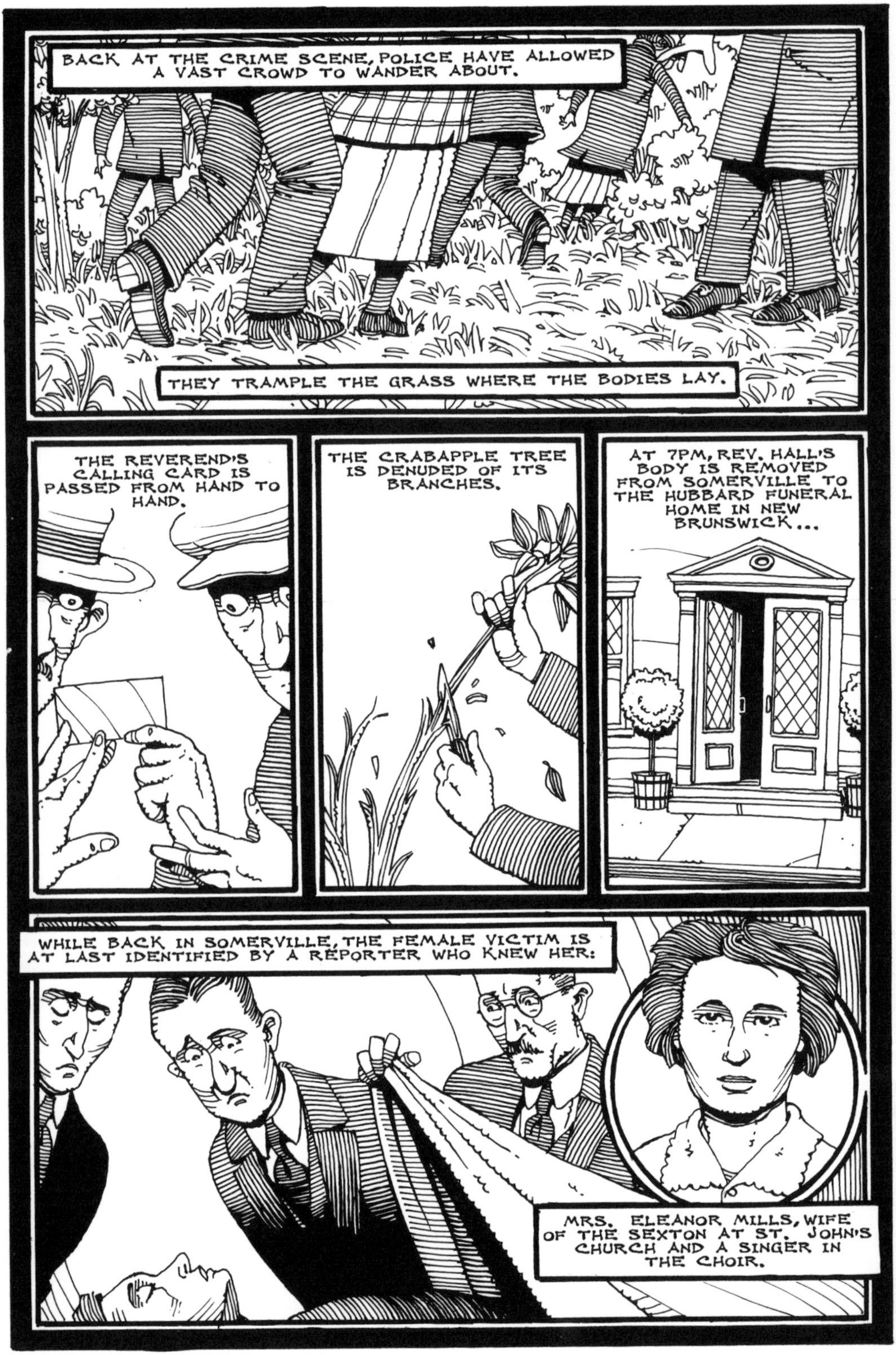
BACK AT THE CRIME SCENE, POLICE HAVE ALLOWED A VAST CROWD TO WANDER ABOUT.
THEY TRAMPLE THE GRASS WHERE THE BODIES LAY.
THE REVEREND'S CALLING CARD IS PASSED FROM HAND TO HAND.
THE CRABAPPLE TREE IS DENUDED OF ITS BRANCHES.
AT 7PM, REV. HALL'S BODY IS REMOVED FROM SOMERVILLE TO THE HUBBARD FUNERAL HOME IN NEW BRUNSWICK...
WHILE BACK IN SOMERVILLE, THE FEMALE VICTIM IS AT LAST IDENTIFIED BY A REPORTER WHO KNEW HER:
MRS. ELEANOR MILLS, WIFE OF THE SEXTON AT ST. JOHN'S CHURCH AND A SINGER IN THE CHOIR.

PART II

THE VICTIMS

THE STORM OF THIS DOUBLE MURDER WILL BE SEEN
TO HAVE ITS CENTER HERE:

THE EPISCOPAL CHURCH OF ST. JOHN THE EVANGELIST
ON GEORGE STREET IN NEW BRUNSWICK.

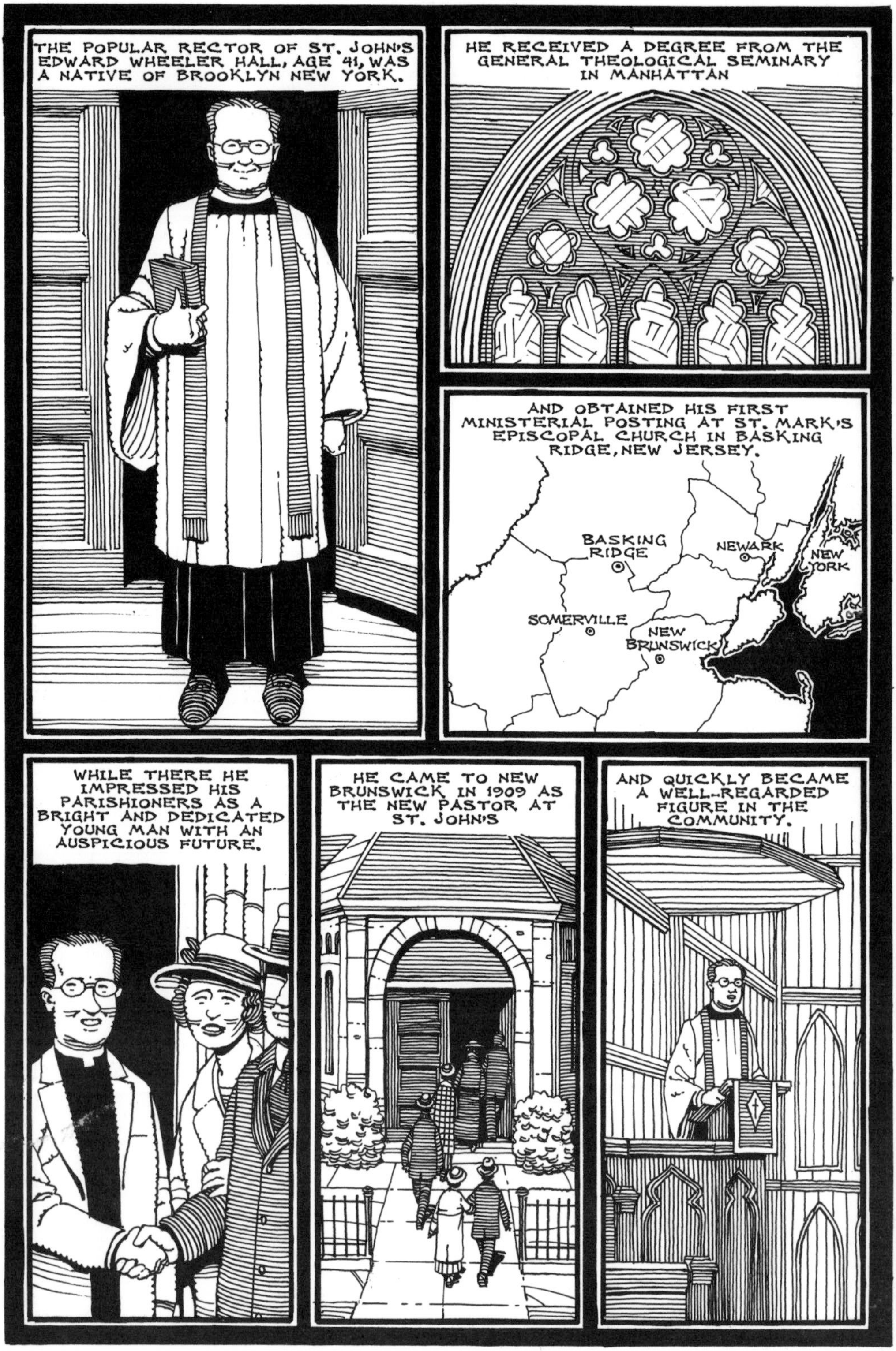
THE POPULAR RECTOR OF ST. JOHN'S EDWARD WHEELER HALL, AGE 41, WAS A NATIVE OF BROOKLYN NEW YORK.
HE RECEIVED A DEGREE FROM THE GENERAL THEOLOGICAL SEMINARY IN MANHATTAN
AND OBTAINED HIS FIRST MINISTERIAL POSTING AT ST. MARK'S EPISCOPAL CHURCH IN BASKING RIDGE, NEW JERSEY.
BASKING RIDGE
NEWARK
NEW YORK
SOMERVILLE
NEW BRUNSWICK
WHILE THERE HE IMPRESSED HIS PARISHIONERS AS A BRIGHT AND DEDICATED YOUNG MAN WITH AN AUSPICIOUS FUTURE.
HE CAME TO NEW BRUNSWICK IN 1909 AS THE NEW PASTOR AT ST. JOHN'S
AND QUICKLY BECAME A WELL-REGARDED FIGURE IN THE COMMUNITY.

IN 1911 HE MARRIED INTO ONE OF NEW BRUNSWICK'S MOST PROMINENT FAMILIES.

FRANCES NOEL STEVENS, ONE OF THE SPINSTERS OF THE CONGREGATION, WAS SEVEN YEARS HIS SENIOR.

SHE ALSO HAPPENED TO BE AN HEIRESS TO THE FORTUNE OF JOHNSON & JOHNSON, THE PHARMACEUTICAL SUPPLY FIRM HEADQUARTERED IN NEW BRUNSWICK.

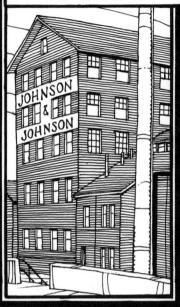

THEY SETTLED INTO HER FAMILY HOME AT 23 NICHOL AVENUE, ON THE EAST SIDE OF TOWN.

LIVING WITH THEM WAS HER ECCENTRIC OLDER BROTHER WILLIE STEVENS.

WILLIE IS A WELL-KNOWN LOCAL "CHARACTER" WHO SUFFERS FROM AN UNSPECIFIED BUT BENIGN MENTAL DISORDER THAT MAKES IT DIFFICULT FOR HIM TO LIVE ON HIS OWN.

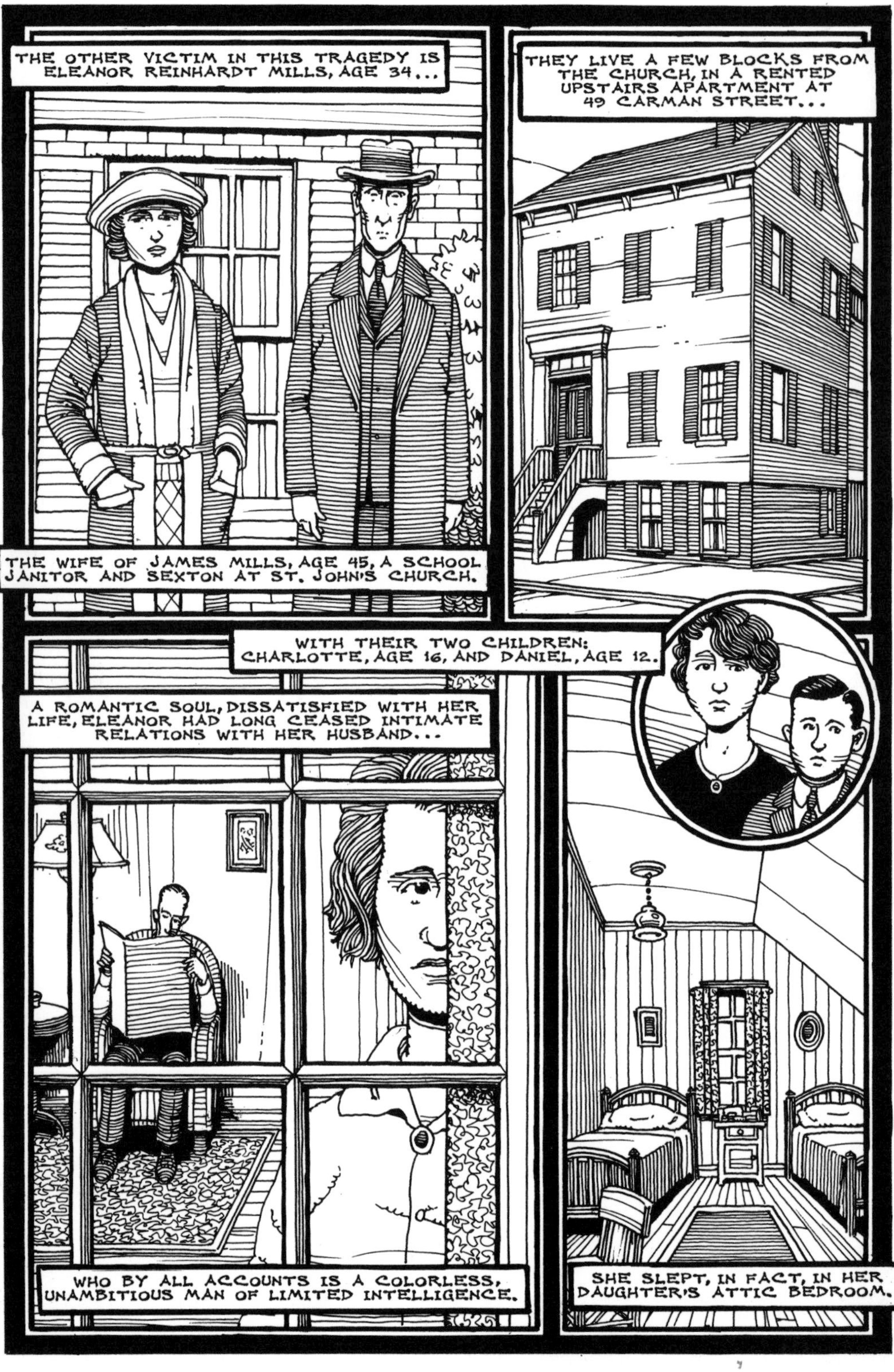
THE OTHER VICTIM IN THIS TRAGEDY IS ELEANOR REINHARDT MILLS, AGE 34...
THE WIFE OF JAMES MILLS, AGE 45, A SCHOOL JANITOR AND SEXTON AT ST. JOHN'S CHURCH.
THEY LIVE A FEW BLOCKS FROM THE CHURCH, IN A RENTED UPSTAIRS APARTMENT AT 49 CARMAN STREET...
WITH THEIR TWO CHILDREN: CHARLOTTE, AGE 16, AND DANIEL, AGE 12.
A ROMANTIC SOUL, DISSATISFIED WITH HER LIFE, ELEANOR HAD LONG CEASED INTIMATE RELATIONS WITH HER HUSBAND...
WHO BY ALL ACCOUNTS IS A COLORLESS, UNAMBITIOUS MAN OF LIMITED INTELLIGENCE.
SHE SLEPT, IN FACT, IN HER DAUGHTER'S ATTIC BEDROOM.

IN CONSEQUENCE, THE CENTER OF ELEANOR'S WORLD BECAME HER WORK AT ST. JOHN'S CHURCH.

SHE WAS A SOPRANO IN THE CHOIR...

AND OFTEN ASSISTED THE REVEREND IN KEEPING HIS OFFICE IN ORDER.

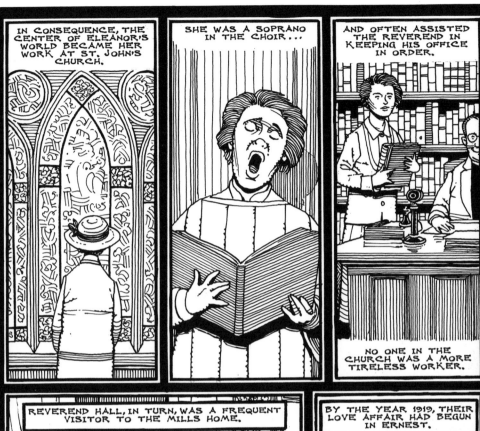

NO ONE IN THE CHURCH WAS A MORE TIRELESS WORKER.

REVEREND HALL, IN TURN, WAS A FREQUENT VISITOR TO THE MILLS HOME.

JAMES MILLS WAS FLATTERED BY THE ATTENTION AND SEEMINGLY BLIND TO THE GROWING ATTRACTION BETWEEN HIS WIFE AND THE MINISTER.

BY THE YEAR 1919, THEIR LOVE AFFAIR HAD BEGUN IN ERNEST.

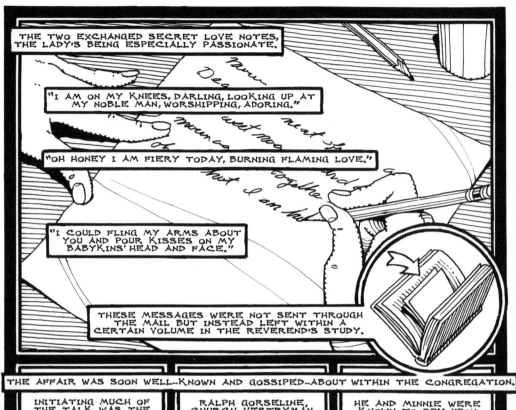

THE TWO EXCHANGED SECRET LOVE NOTES, THE LADY'S BEING ESPECIALLY PASSIONATE.

"I AM ON MY KNEES, DARLING, LOOKING UP AT MY NOBLE MAN, WORSHIPPING, ADORING."

"OH HONEY I AM FIERY TODAY, BURNING FLAMING LOVE."

"I COULD FLING MY ARMS ABOUT YOU AND POUR KISSES ON MY BABYKINS' HEAD AND FACE."

THESE MESSAGES WERE NOT SENT THROUGH THE MAIL BUT INSTEAD LEFT WITHIN A CERTAIN VOLUME IN THE REVEREND'S STUDY.

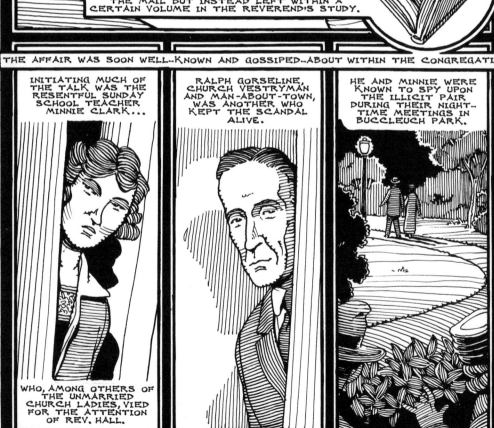

THE AFFAIR WAS SOON WELL-KNOWN AND GOSSIPED-ABOUT WITHIN THE CONGREGATION.

INITIATING MUCH OF THE TALK WAS THE RESENTFUL SUNDAY SCHOOL TEACHER MINNIE CLARK...

WHO, AMONG OTHERS OF THE UNMARRIED CHURCH LADIES, VIED FOR THE ATTENTION OF REV. HALL.

RALPH GORSELINE, CHURCH VESTRYMAN AND MAN-ABOUT-TOWN, WAS ANOTHER WHO KEPT THE SCANDAL ALIVE.

HE AND MINNIE WERE KNOWN TO SPY UPON THE ILLICIT PAIR DURING THEIR NIGHT-TIME MEETINGS IN BUCCLEUCH PARK.

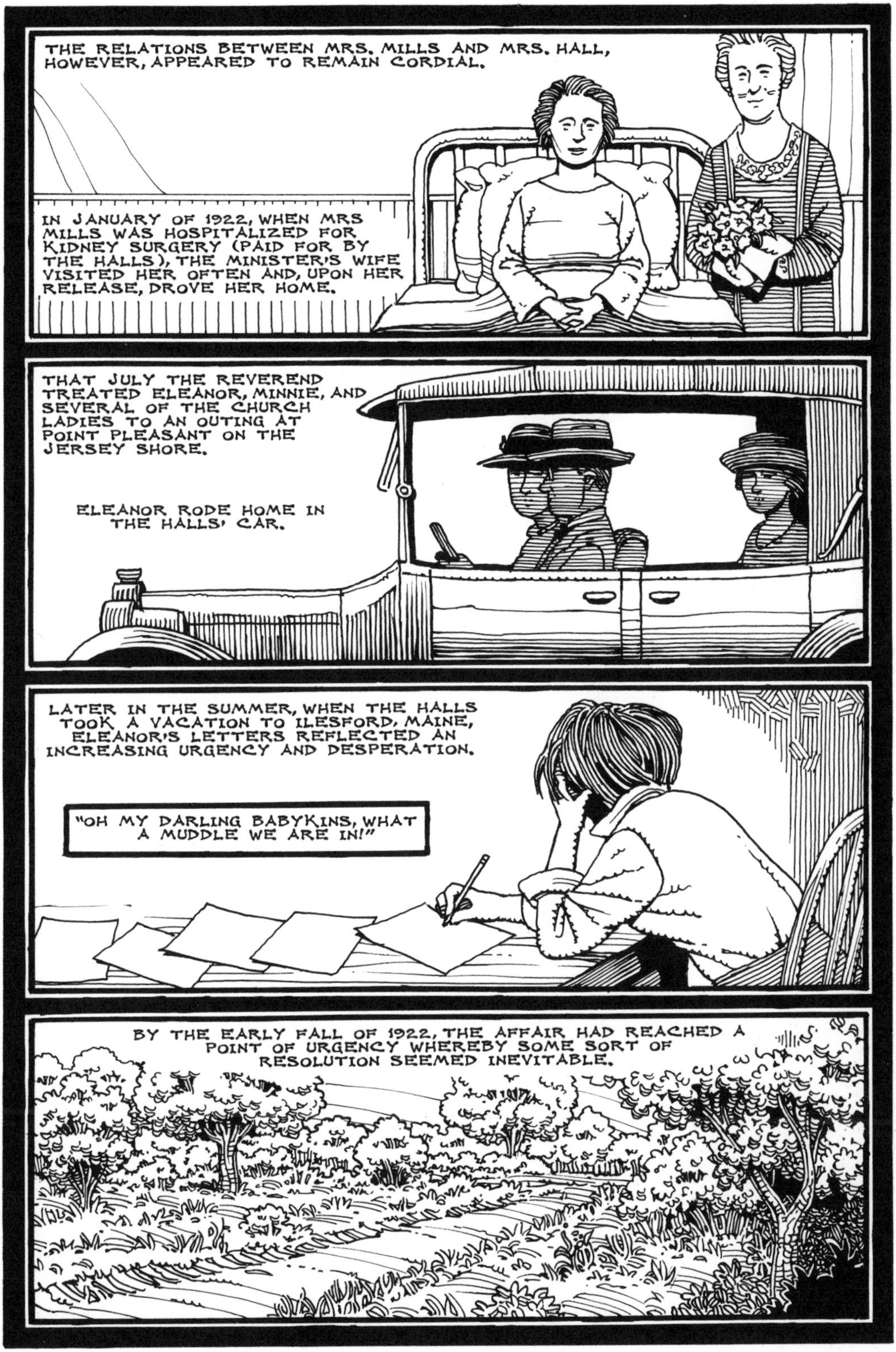
THE RELATIONS BETWEEN MRS. MILLS AND MRS. HALL, HOWEVER, APPEARED TO REMAIN CORDIAL.
IN JANUARY OF 1922, WHEN MRS MILLS WAS HOSPITALIZED FOR KIDNEY SURGERY (PAID FOR BY THE HALLS), THE MINISTER'S WIFE VISITED HER OFTEN AND, UPON HER RELEASE, DROVE HER HOME.
THAT JULY THE REVEREND TREATED ELEANOR, MINNIE, AND SEVERAL OF THE CHURCH LADIES TO AN OUTING AT POINT PLEASANT ON THE JERSEY SHORE.
ELEANOR RODE HOME IN THE HALLS' CAR.
LATER IN THE SUMMER, WHEN THE HALLS TOOK A VACATION TO ILESFORD, MAINE, ELEANOR'S LETTERS REFLECTED AN INCREASING URGENCY AND DESPERATION.
"OH MY DARLING BABYKINS, WHAT A MUDDLE WE ARE IN!"
BY THE EARLY FALL OF 1922, THE AFFAIR HAD REACHED A POINT OF URGENCY WHEREBY SOME SORT OF RESOLUTION SEEMED INEVITABLE.

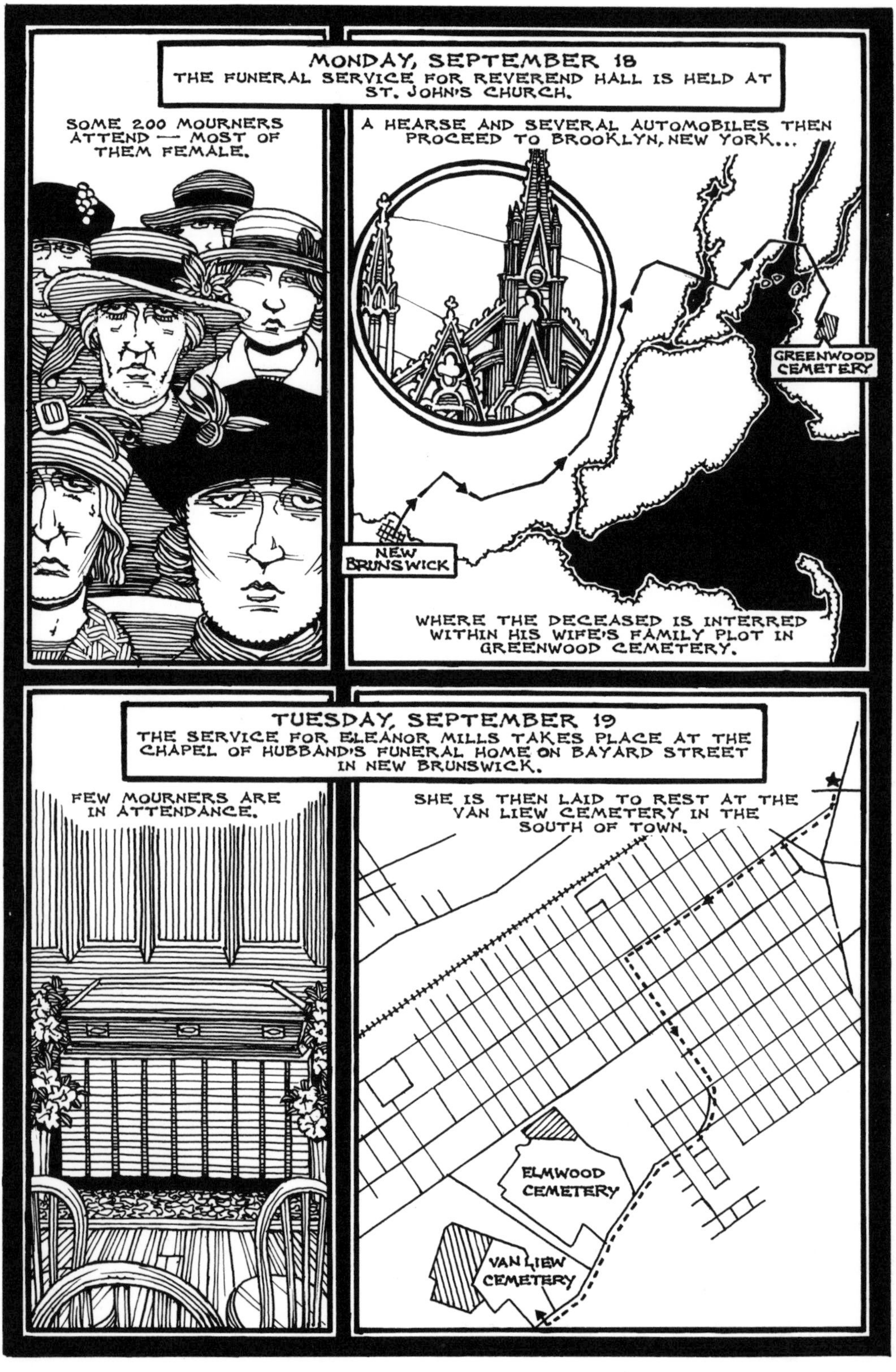

MONDAY, SEPTEMBER 18
THE FUNERAL SERVICE FOR REVEREND HALL IS HELD AT ST. JOHN'S CHURCH.
SOME 200 MOURNERS ATTEND — MOST OF THEM FEMALE.
A HEARSE AND SEVERAL AUTOMOBILES THEN PROCEED TO BROOKLYN, NEW YORK...
GREENWOOD CEMETERY
NEW BRUNSWICK
WHERE THE DECEASED IS INTERRED WITHIN HIS WIFE'S FAMILY PLOT IN GREENWOOD CEMETERY.
TUESDAY, SEPTEMBER 19
THE SERVICE FOR ELEANOR MILLS TAKES PLACE AT THE CHAPEL OF HUBBAND'S FUNERAL HOME ON BAYARD STREET IN NEW BRUNSWICK.
FEW MOURNERS ARE IN ATTENDANCE.
SHE IS THEN LAID TO REST AT THE VAN LIEW CEMETERY IN THE SOUTH OF TOWN.
ELMWOOD CEMETERY
VAN LIEW CEMETERY

PART III

THE SEARCH
FOR EVIDENCE

NEW BRUNSWICK POLICE, WHO BELIEVE THAT THE CRIME
WILL BE SOLVED QUICKLY, ATTEMPT TO PIECE
TOGETHER THE VICTIMS' FINAL HOURS.

BUT THE INVESTIGATION BEGINS WITH A
BUILT-IN CONFLICT.

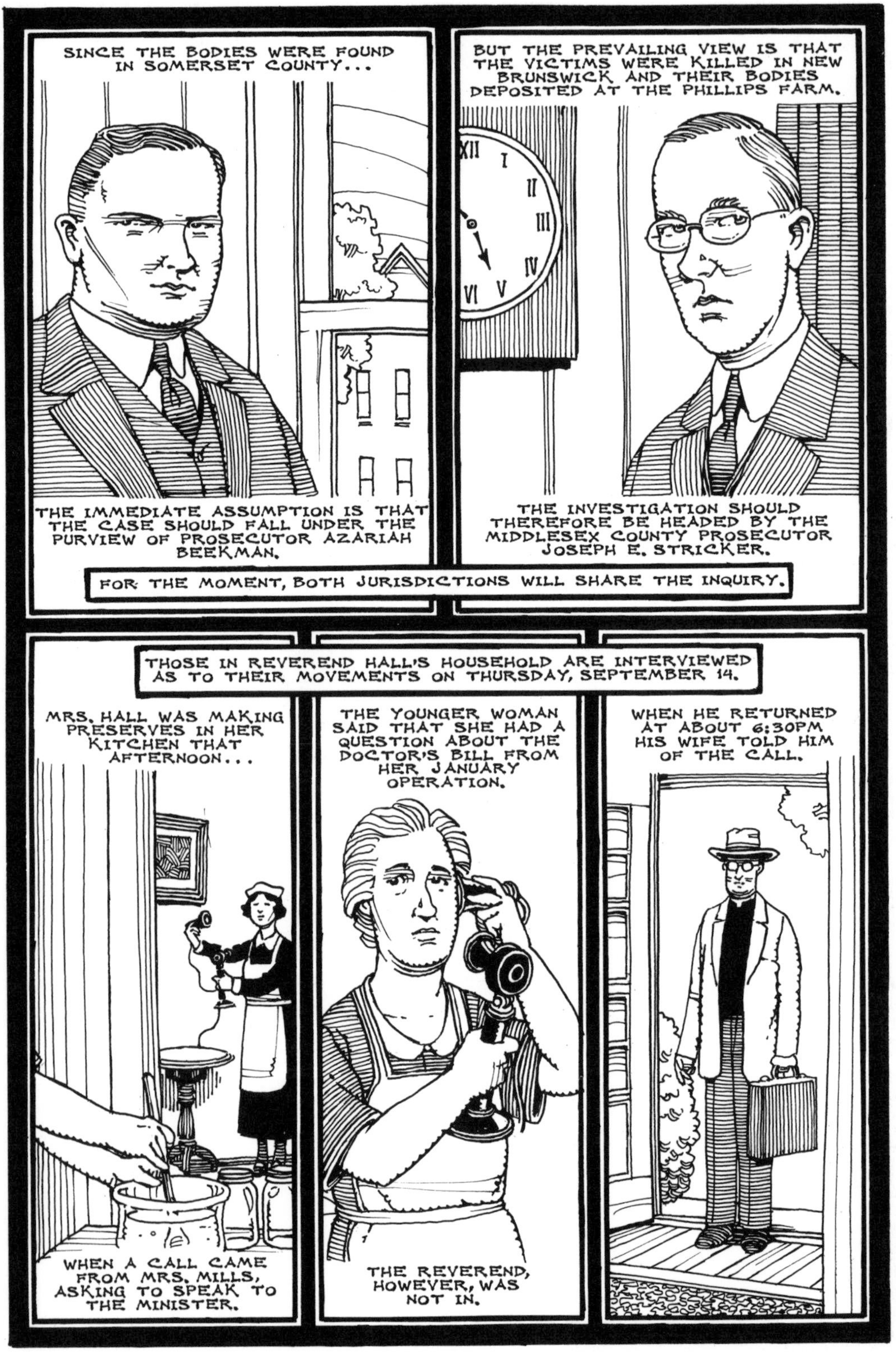
SINCE THE BODIES WERE FOUND IN SOMERSET COUNTY...
THE IMMEDIATE ASSUMPTION IS THAT THE CASE SHOULD FALL UNDER THE PURVIEW OF PROSECUTOR AZARIAH BEEKMAN.
BUT THE PREVAILING VIEW IS THAT THE VICTIMS WERE KILLED IN NEW BRUNSWICK AND THEIR BODIES DEPOSITED AT THE PHILLIPS FARM.
THE INVESTIGATION SHOULD THEREFORE BE HEADED BY THE MIDDLESEX COUNTY PROSECUTOR JOSEPH E. STRICKER.
FOR THE MOMENT, BOTH JURISDICTIONS WILL SHARE THE INQUIRY.
THOSE IN REVEREND HALL'S HOUSEHOLD ARE INTERVIEWED AS TO THEIR MOVEMENTS ON THURSDAY, SEPTEMBER 14.
MRS. HALL WAS MAKING PRESERVES IN HER KITCHEN THAT AFTERNOON...
WHEN A CALL CAME FROM MRS. MILLS, ASKING TO SPEAK TO THE MINISTER.
THE YOUNGER WOMAN SAID THAT SHE HAD A QUESTION ABOUT THE DOCTOR'S BILL FROM HER JANUARY OPERATION.
THE REVEREND, HOWEVER, WAS NOT IN.
WHEN HE RETURNED AT ABOUT 6:30PM HIS WIFE TOLD HIM OF THE CALL.

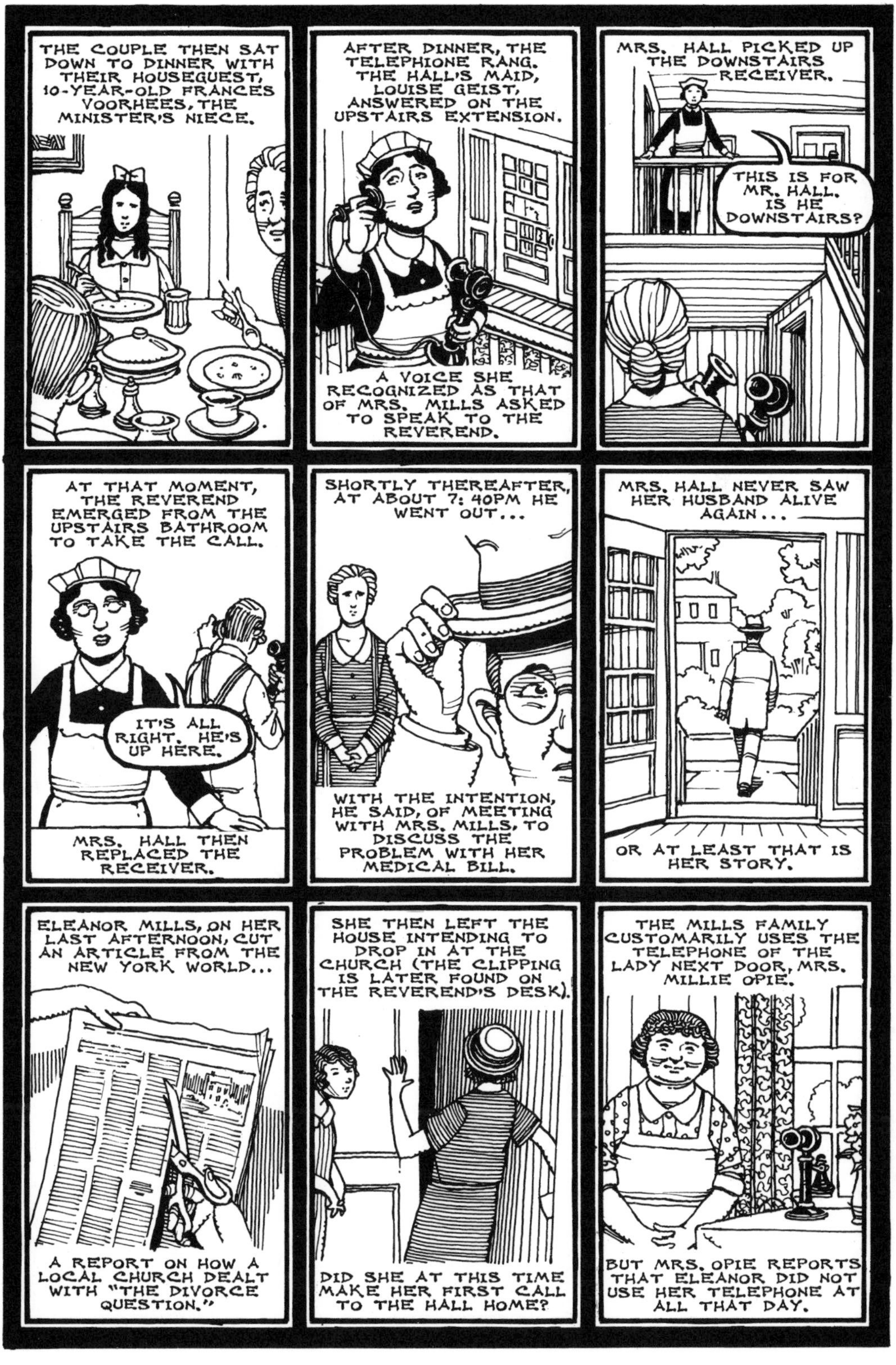
THE COUPLE THEN SAT DOWN TO DINNER WITH THEIR HOUSEGUEST, 10-YEAR-OLD FRANCES VOORHEES, THE MINISTER'S NIECE.
AFTER DINNER, THE TELEPHIONE RANG. THE HALL'S MAID, LOUISE GEIST, ANSWERED ON THE UPSTAIRS EXTENSION.
A VOICE SHE RECOGNIZED AS THAT OF MRS. MILLS ASKED TO SPEAK TO THE REVEREND.
MRS. HALL PICKED UP THE DOWNSTAIRS RECEIVER.
THIS IS FOR MR. HALL. IS HE DOWNSTAIRS?
AT THAT MOMENT, THE REVEREND EMERGED FROM THE UPSTAIRS BATHROOM TO TAKE THE CALL.
IT'S ALL RIGHT. HE'S UP HERE.
MRS. HALL THEN REPLACED THE RECEIVER.
SHORTLY THEREAFTER, AT ABOUT 7:40PM HE WENT OUT...
WITH THE INTENTION, HE SAID, OF MEETING WITH MRS. MILLS, TO DISCUSS THE PROBLEM WITH HER MEDICAL BILL.
MRS. HALL NEVER SAW HER HUSBAND ALIVE AGAIN...
OR AT LEAST THAT IS HER STORY.
ELEANOR MILLS, ON HER LAST AFTERNOON, CUT AN ARTICLE FROM THE NEW YORK WORLD...
A REPORT ON HOW A LOCAL CHURCH DEALT WITH "THE DIVORCE QUESTION."
SHE THEN LEFT THE HOUSE INTENDING TO DROP IN AT THE CHURCH (THE CLIPPING IS LATER FOUND ON THE REVEREND'S DESK).
DID SHE AT THIS TIME MAKE HER FIRST CALL TO THE HALL HOME?
THE MILLS FAMILY CUSTOMARILY USES THE TELEPHONE OF THE LADY NEXT DOOR, MRS. MILLIE OPIE.
BUT MRS. OPIE REPORTS THAT ELEANOR DID NOT USE HER TELEPHONE AT ALL THAT DAY.

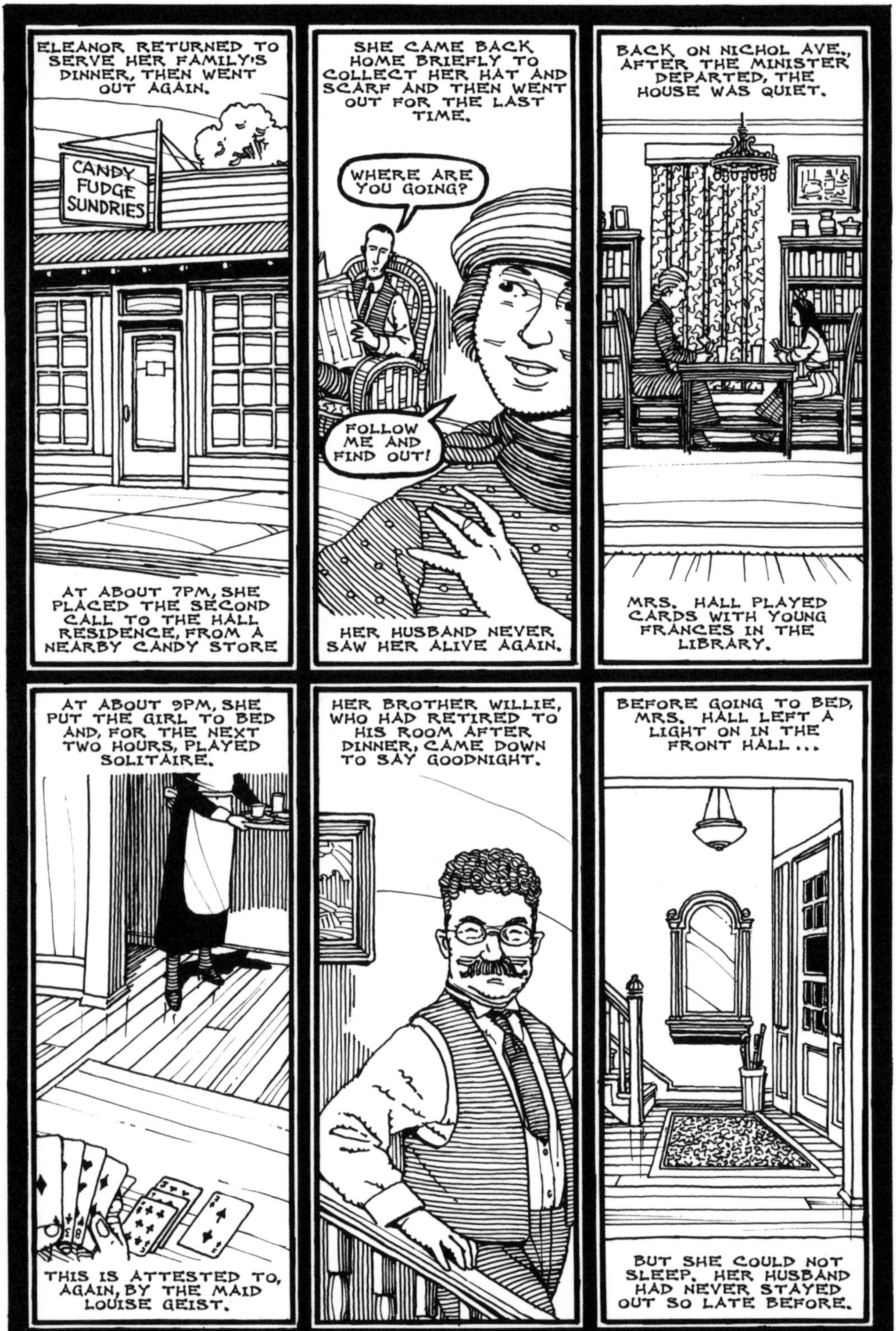
ELEANOR RETURNED TO SERVE HER FAMILY'S DINNER, THEN WENT OUT AGAIN.
CANDY FUDGE SUNDRIES
AT ABOUT 7PM, SHE PLACED THE SECOND CALL TO THE HALL RESIDENCE, FROM A NEARBY CANDY STORE
SHE CAME BACK HOME BRIEFLY TO COLLECT HER HAT AND SCARF AND THEN WENT OUT FOR THE LAST TIME.
WHERE ARE YOU GOING?
FOLLOW ME AND FIND OUT!
HER HUSBAND NEVER SAW HER ALIVE AGAIN.
BACK ON NICHOL AVE., AFTER THE MINISTER DEPARTED, THE HOUSE WAS QUIET.
MRS. HALL PLAYED CARDS WITH YOUNG FRANCES IN THE LIBRARY.
AT ABOUT 9PM, SHE PUT THE GIRL TO BED AND, FOR THE NEXT TWO HOURS, PLAYED SOLITAIRE.
THIS IS ATTESTED TO, AGAIN, BY THE MAID LOUISE GEIST.
HER BROTHER WILLIE, WHO HAD RETIRED TO HIS ROOM AFTER DINNER, CAME DOWN TO SAY GOODNIGHT.
BEFORE GOING TO BED, MRS. HALL LEFT A LIGHT ON IN THE FRONT HALL...
BUT SHE COULD NOT SLEEP. HER HUSBAND HAD NEVER STAYED OUT SO LATE BEFORE.

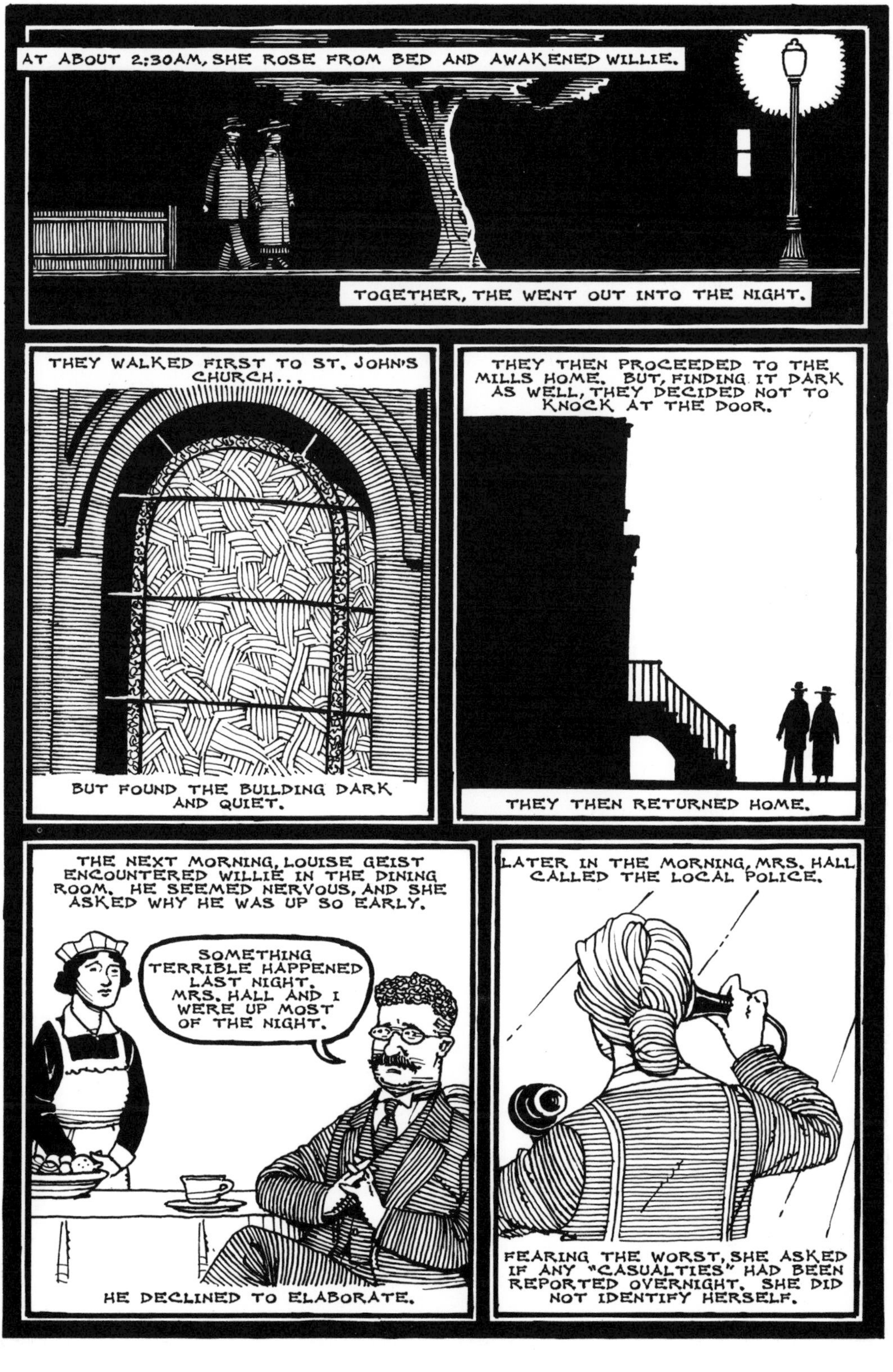
AT ABOUT 2:30AM, SHE ROSE FROM BED AND AWAKENED WILLIE.
TOGETHER, THE WENT OUT INTO THE NIGHT.
THEY WALKED FIRST TO ST. JOHN'S CHURCH...
BUT FOUND THE BUILDING DARK AND QUIET.
THEY THEN PROCEEDED TO THE MILLS HOME. BUT, FINDING IT DARK AS WELL, THEY DECIDED NOT TO KNOCK AT THE DOOR.
THEY THEN RETURNED HOME.
THE NEXT MORNING, LOUISE GEIST ENCOUNTERED WILLIE IN THE DINING ROOM. HE SEEMED NERVOUS, AND SHE ASKED WHY HE WAS UP SO EARLY.
SOMETHING TERRIBLE HAPPENED LAST NIGHT. MRS. HALL AND I WERE UP MOST OF THE NIGHT.
HE DECLINED TO ELABORATE.
LATER IN THE MORNING, MRS. HALL CALLED THE LOCAL POLICE.
FEARING THE WORST, SHE ASKED IF ANY "CASUALTIES" HAD BEEN REPORTED OVERNIGHT. SHE DID NOT IDENTIFY HERSELF.

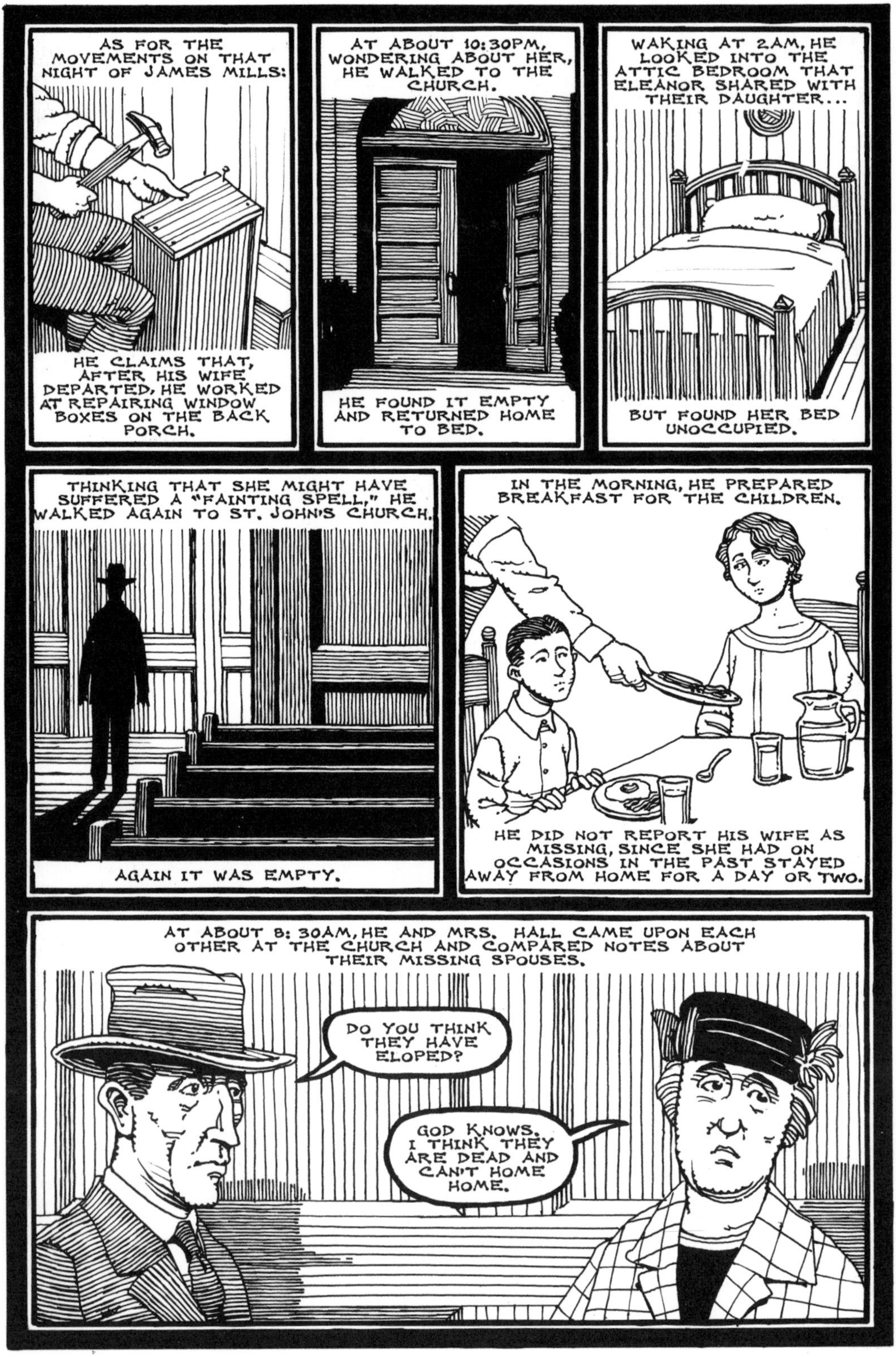
AS FOR THE MOVEMENTS ON THAT NIGHT OF JAMES MILLS:
HE CLAIMS THAT, AFTER HIS WIFE DEPARTED, HE WORKED AT REPAIRING WINDOW BOXES ON THE BACK PORCH.
AT ABOUT 10:30PM, WONDERING ABOUT HER, HE WALKED TO THE CHURCH.
HE FOUND IT EMPTY AND RETURNED HOME TO BED.
WAKING AT 2AM, HE LOOKED INTO THE ATTIC BEDROOM THAT ELEANOR SHARED WITH THEIR DAUGHTER...
BUT FOUND HER BED UNOCCUPIED.
THINKING THAT SHE MIGHT HAVE SUFFERED A "FAINTING SPELL," HE WALKED AGAIN TO ST. JOHN'S CHURCH.
AGAIN IT WAS EMPTY.
IN THE MORNING, HE PREPARED BREAKFAST FOR THE CHILDREN.
HE DID NOT REPORT HIS WIFE AS MISSING, SINCE SHE HAD ON OCCASIONS IN THE PAST STAYED AWAY FROM HOME FOR A DAY OR TWO.
AT ABOUT 8:30AM, HE AND MRS. HALL CAME UPON EACH OTHER AT THE CHURCH AND COMPARED NOTES ABOUT THEIR MISSING SPOUSES.
DO YOU THINK THEY HAVE ELOPED?
GOD KNOWS. I THINK THEY ARE DEAD AND CAN'T HOME HOME.

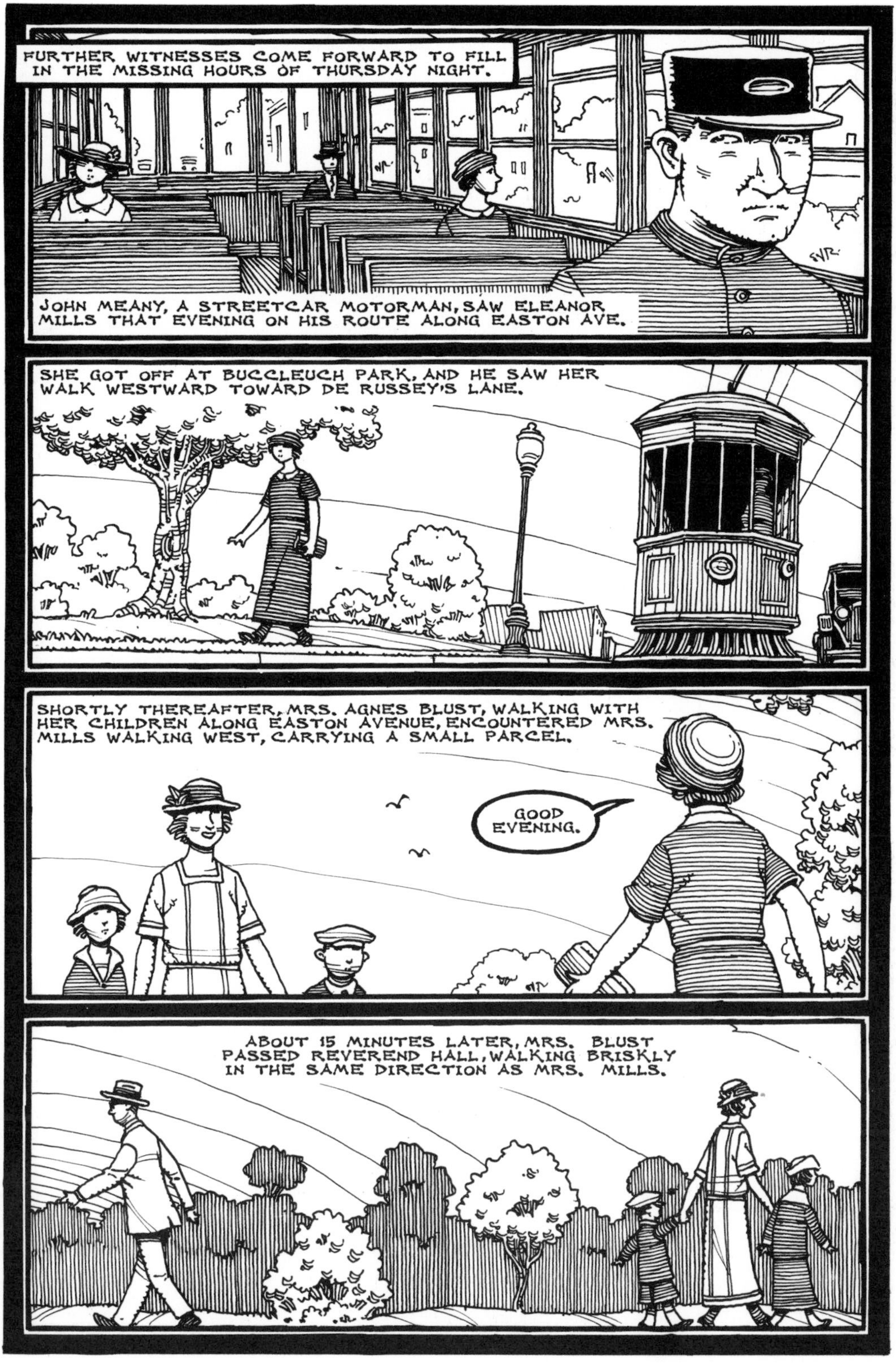
FURTHER WITNESSES COME FORWARD TO FILL IN THE MISSING HOURS OF THURSDAY NIGHT.
SVR
JOHN MEANY, A STREETCAR MOTORMAN, SAW ELEANOR MILLS THAT EVENING ON HIS ROUTE ALONG EASTON AVE.
SHE GOT OFF AT BUCCLEUCH PARK, AND HE SAW HER WALK WESTWARD TOWARD DE RUSSEY'S LANE.
SHORTLY THEREAFTER, MRS. AGNES BLUST, WALKING WITH HER CHILDREN ALONG EASTON AVENUE, ENCOUNTERED MRS. MILLS WALKING WEST, CARRYING A SMALL PARCEL.
GOOD EVENING.
ABOUT 15 MINUTES LATER, MRS. BLUST PASSED REVEREND HALL, WALKING BRISKLY IN THE SAME DIRECTION AS MRS. MILLS.

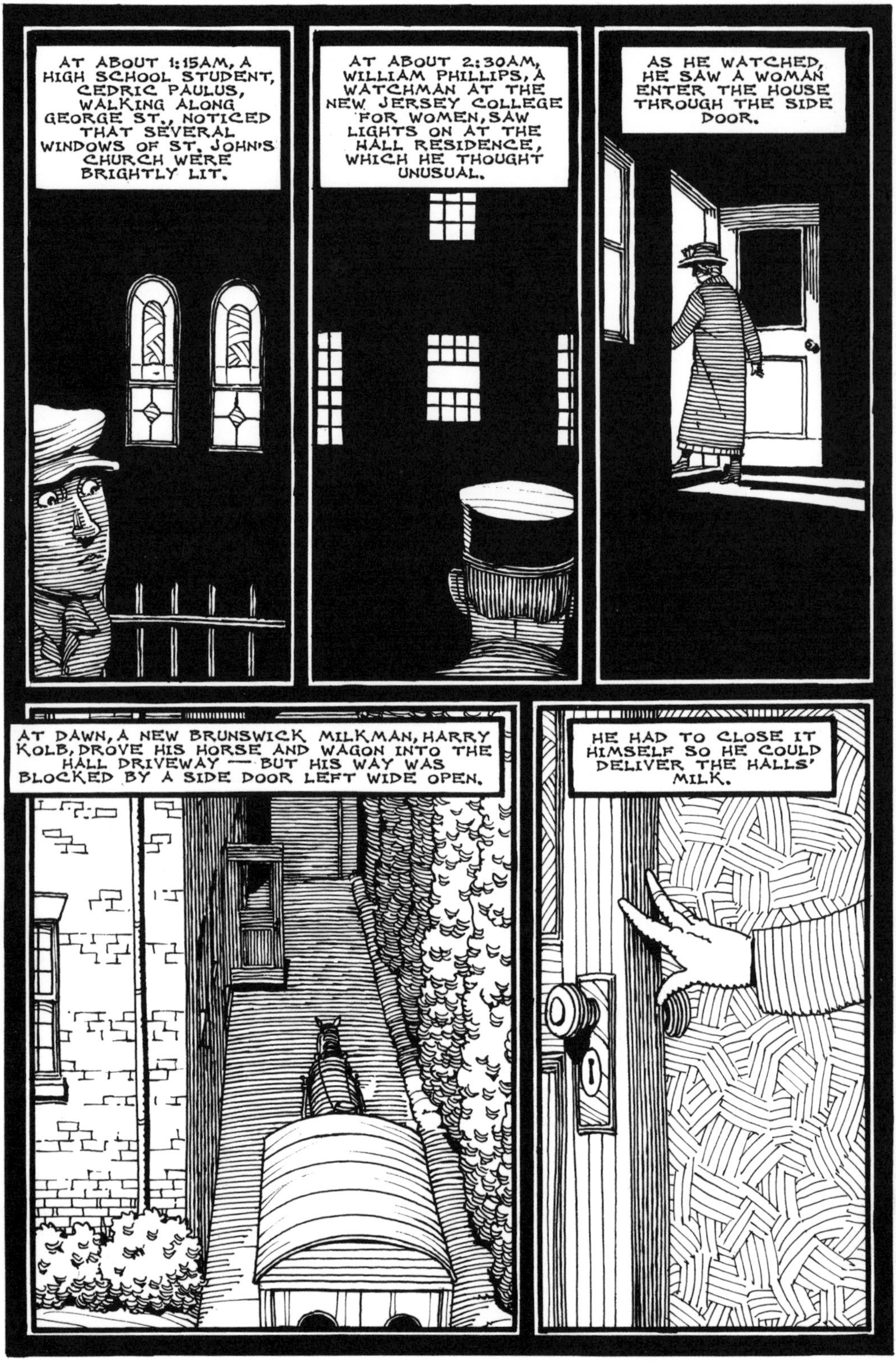
AT ABOUT 1:15AM, A HIGH SCHOOL STUDENT, CEDRIC PAULUS, WALKING ALONG GEORGE ST., NOTICED THAT SEVERAL WINDOWS OF ST. JOHN'S CHURCH WERE BRIGHTLY LIT.
AT ABOUT 2:30AM, WILLIAM PHILLIPS, A WATCHMAN AT THE NEW JERSEY COLLEGE FOR WOMEN, SAW LIGHTS ON AT THE HALL RESIDENCE, WHICH HE THOUGHT UNUSUAL.
AS HE WATCHED, HE SAW A WOMAN ENTER THE HOUSE THROUGH THE SIDE DOOR.
AT DAWN, A NEW BRUNSWICK MILKMAN, HARRY KOLB, DROVE HIS HORSE AND WAGON INTO THE HALL DRIVEWAY — BUT HIS WAY WAS BLOCKED BY A SIDE DOOR LEFT WIDE OPEN.
HE HAD TO CLOSE IT HIMSELF SO HE COULD DELIVER THE HALLS' MILK.

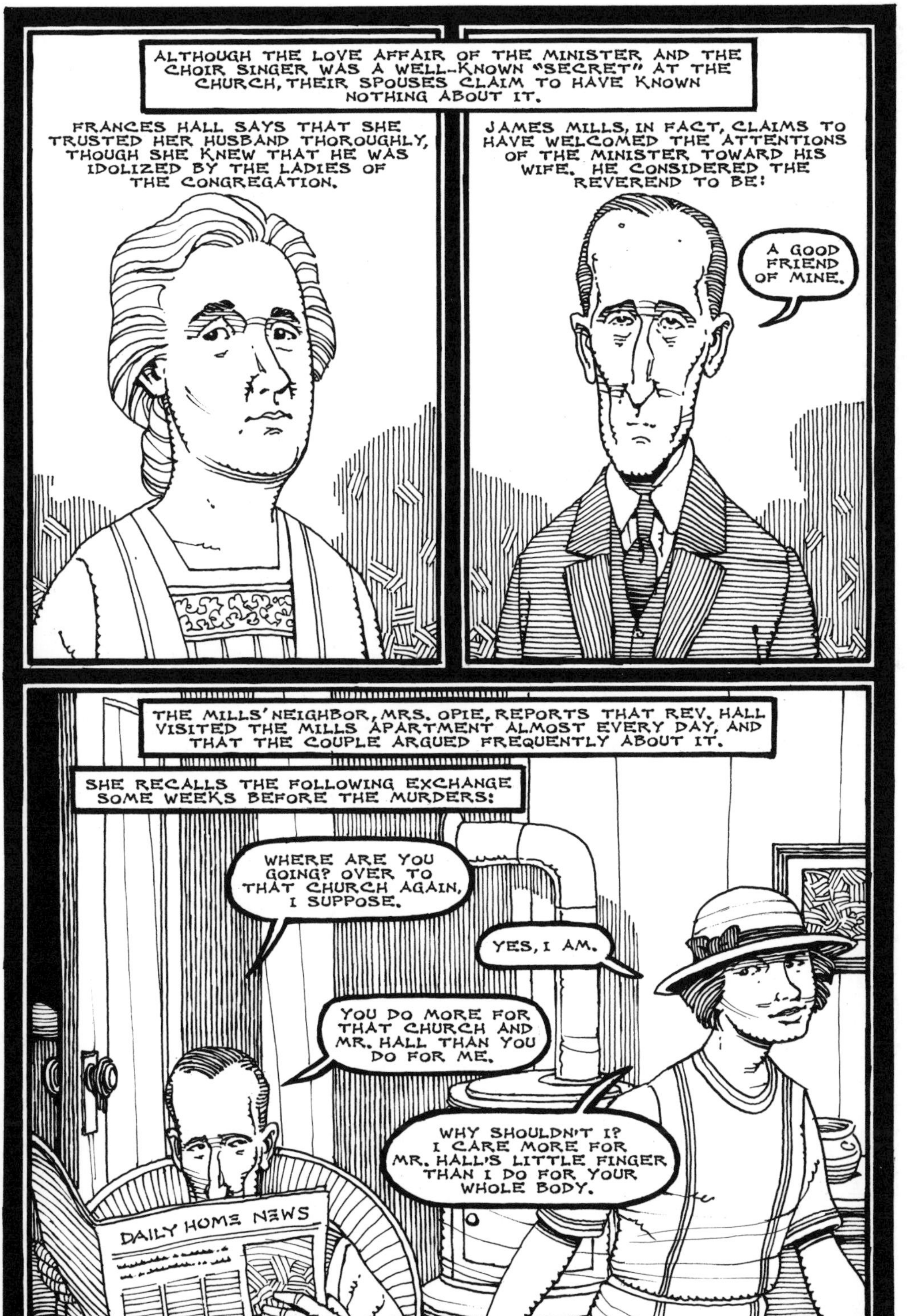
ALTHOUGH THE LOVE AFFAIR OF THE MINISTER AND THE CHOIR SINGER WAS A WELL-KNOWN "SECRET" AT THE CHURCH, THEIR SPOUSES CLAIM TO HAVE KNOWN NOTHING ABOUT IT.
FRANCES HALL SAYS THAT SHE TRUSTED HER HUSBAND THOROUGHLY, THOUGH SHE KNEW THAT HE WAS IDOLIZED BY THE LADIES OF THE CONGREGATION.
JAMES MILLS, IN FACT, CLAIMS TO HAVE WELCOMED THE ATTENTIONS OF THE MINISTER TOWARD HIS WIFE. HE CONSIDERED THE REVEREND TO BE:
A GOOD FRIEND OF MINE.
THE MILLS' NEIGHBOR, MRS. OPIE, REPORTS THAT REV. HALL VISITED THE MILLS APARTMENT ALMOST EVERY DAY, AND THAT THE COUPLE ARGUED FREQUENTLY ABOUT IT.
SHE RECALLS THE FOLLOWING EXCHANGE SOME WEEKS BEFORE THE MURDERS:
WHERE ARE YOU GOING? OVER TO THAT CHURCH AGAIN, I SUPPOSE.
YES, I AM.
YOU DO MORE FOR THAT CHURCH AND MR. HALL THAN YOU DO FOR ME.
WHY SHOULDN'T I? I CARE MORE FOR MR. HALL'S LITTLE FINGER THAN I DO FOR YOUR WHOLE BODY.
DAILY HOME NEWS

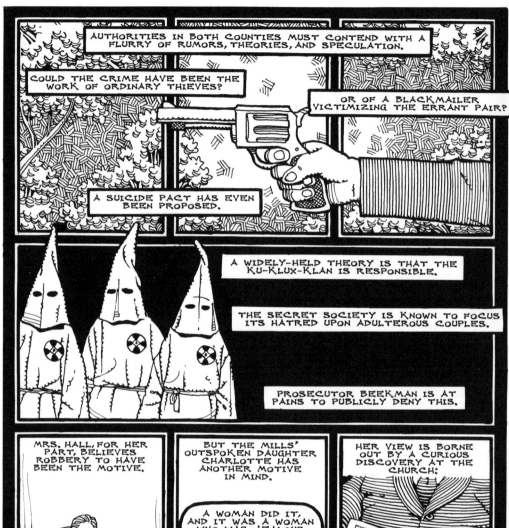

AUTHORITIES IN BOTH COUNTIES MUST CONTEND WITH A FLURRY OF RUMORS, THEORIES, AND SPECULATION.

COULD THE CRIME HAVE BEEN THE WORK OF ORDINARY THIEVES?

OR OF A BLACKMAILER VICTIMIZING THE ERRANT PAIR?

A SUICIDE PACT HAS EVEN BEEN PROPOSED.

A WIDELY-HELD THEORY IS THAT THE KU-KLUX-KLAN IS RESPONSIBLE.

THE SECRET SOCIETY IS KNOWN TO FOCUS ITS HATRED UPON ADULTEROUS COUPLES.

PROSECUTOR BEEKMAN IS AT PAINS TO PUBLICLY DENY THIS.

MRS. HALL, FOR HER PART, BELIEVES ROBBERY TO HAVE BEEN THE MOTIVE.

HER HUSBAND'S GOLD POCKET WATCH AND $50 IN CASH APPEAR TO BE MISSING.

BUT THE MILLS' OUTSPOKEN DAUGHTER CHARLOTTE HAS ANOTHER MOTIVE IN MIND.

A WOMAN DID IT, AND IT WAS A WOMAN WHO WAS JEALOUS OF MY MOTHER AND WANTED REVENGE.

HER VIEW IS BORNE OUT BY A CURIOUS DISCOVERY AT THE CHURCH:

ELEANOR MILLS' FAVORITE SONG, "PEACE, PERFECT PEACE," HAS BEEN TORN FROM EVERY HYMNAL.

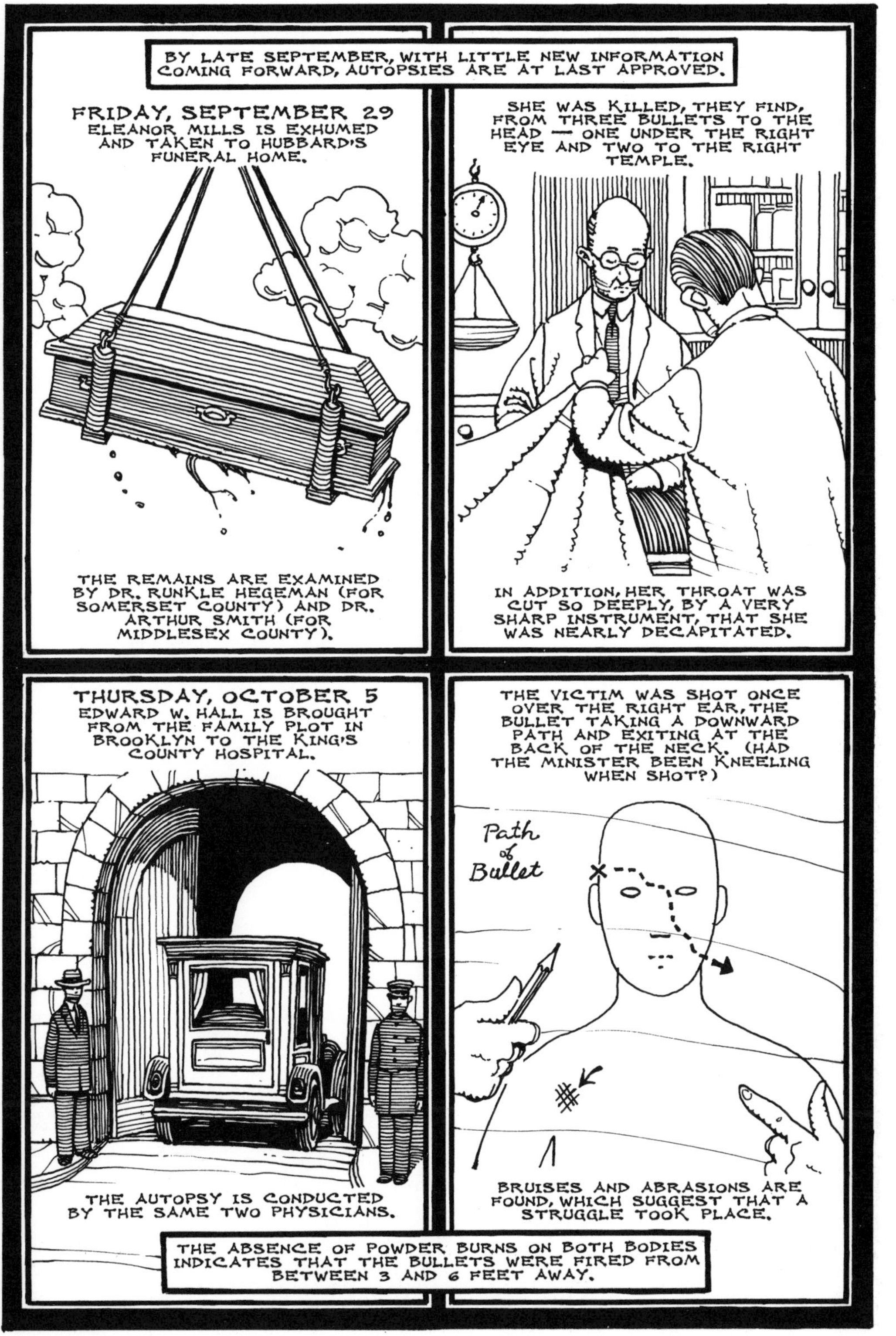
BY LATE SEPTEMBER, WITH LITTLE NEW INFORMATION COMING FORWARD, AUTOPSIES ARE AT LAST APPROVED.
FRIDAY, SEPTEMBER 29
ELEANOR MILLS IS EXHUMED AND TAKEN TO HUBBARD'S FUNERAL HOME.
THE REMAINS ARE EXAMINED BY DR. RUNKLE HEGEMAN (FOR SOMERSET COUNTY) AND DR. ARTHUR SMITH (FOR MIDDLESEX COUNTY).
SHE WAS KILLED, THEY FIND, FROM THREE BULLETS TO THE HEAD — ONE UNDER THE RIGHT EYE AND TWO TO THE RIGHT TEMPLE.
IN ADDITION, HER THROAT WAS CUT SO DEEPLY, BY A VERY SHARP INSTRUMENT, THAT SHE WAS NEARLY DECAPITATED.
THURSDAY, OCTOBER 5
EDWARD W. HALL IS BROUGHT FROM THE FAMILY PLOT IN BROOKLYN TO THE KING'S COUNTY HOSPITAL.
THE AUTOPSY IS CONDUCTED BY THE SAME TWO PHYSICIANS.
THE VICTIM WAS SHOT ONCE OVER THE RIGHT EAR, THE BULLET TAKING A DOWNWARD PATH AND EXITING AT THE BACK OF THE NECK. (HAD THE MINISTER BEEN KNEELING WHEN SHOT?)
Path of Bullet
BRUISES AND ABRASIONS ARE FOUND, WHICH SUGGEST THAT A STRUGGLE TOOK PLACE.
THE ABSENCE OF POWDER BURNS ON BOTH BODIES INDICATES THAT THE BULLETS WERE FIRED FROM BETWEEN 3 AND 6 FEET AWAY.

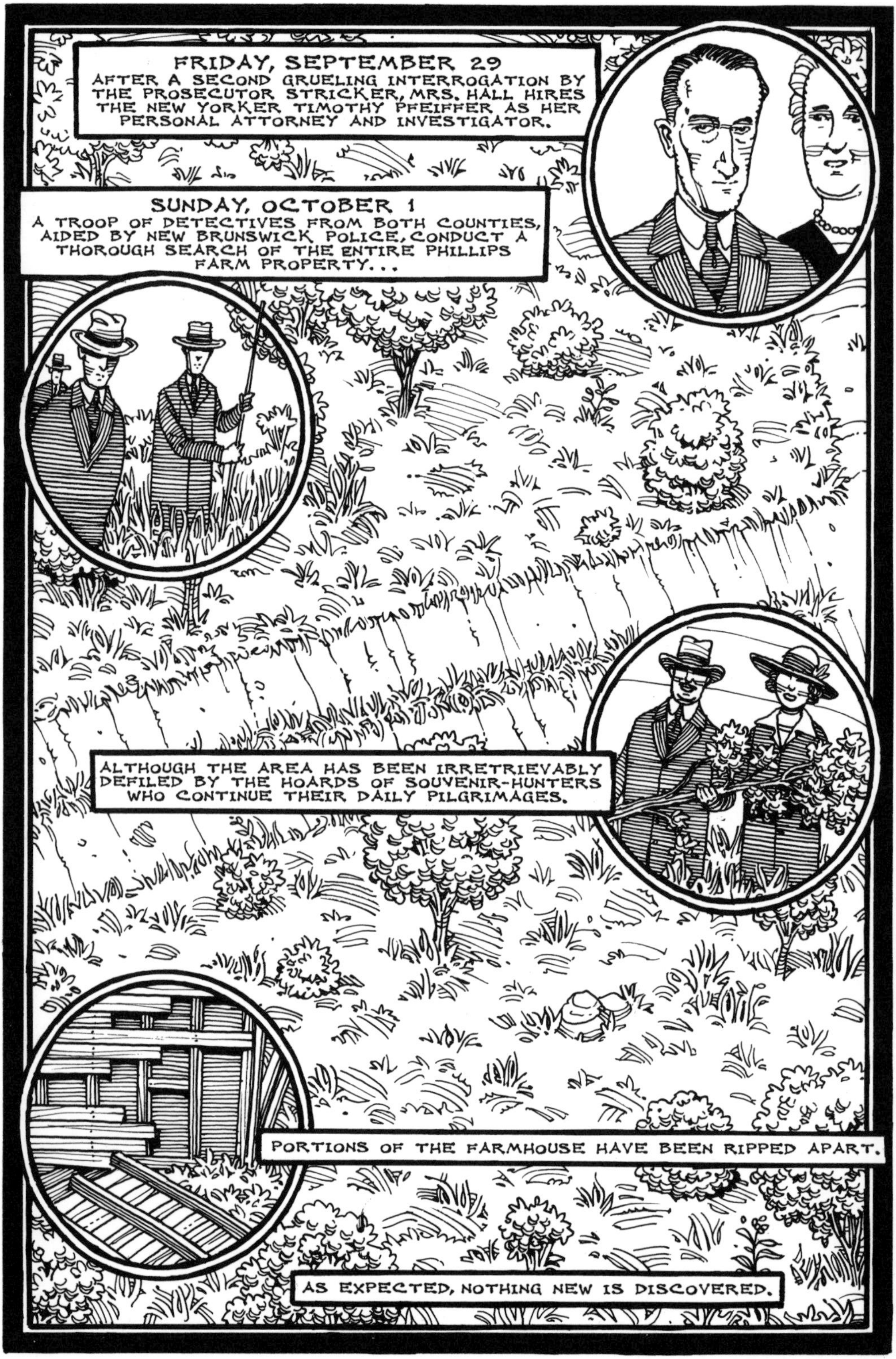
FRIDAY, SEPTEMBER 29
AFTER A SECOND GRUELING INTERROGATION BY THE PROSECUTOR STRICKER, MRS. HALL HIRES THE NEW YORKER TIMOTHY PFEIFFER AS HER PERSONAL ATTORNEY AND INVESTIGATOR.
SUNDAY, OCTOBER 1
A TROOP OF DETECTIVES FROM BOTH COUNTIES, AIDED BY NEW BRUNSWICK POLICE, CONDUCT A THOROUGH SEARCH OF THE ENTIRE PHILLIPS FARM PROPERTY...
ALTHOUGH THE AREA HAS BEEN IRRETRIEVABLY DEFILED BY THE HOARDS OF SOUVENIR-HUNTERS WHO CONTINUE THEIR DAILY PILGRIMAGES.
PORTIONS OF THE FARMHOUSE HAVE BEEN RIPPED APART.
AS EXPECTED, NOTHING NEW IS DISCOVERED.

PART IV

THE CASE TO NOWHERE

SUNDAY, OCTOBER 8
FOUR YOUNG PEOPLE ARE BROUGHT TO THE MIDDLESEX
PROSECUTOR'S OFFICE FOR INTERROGATION...

AND THE LANGUISHING INVESTIGATION SPRINGS
BACK TO LIFE.

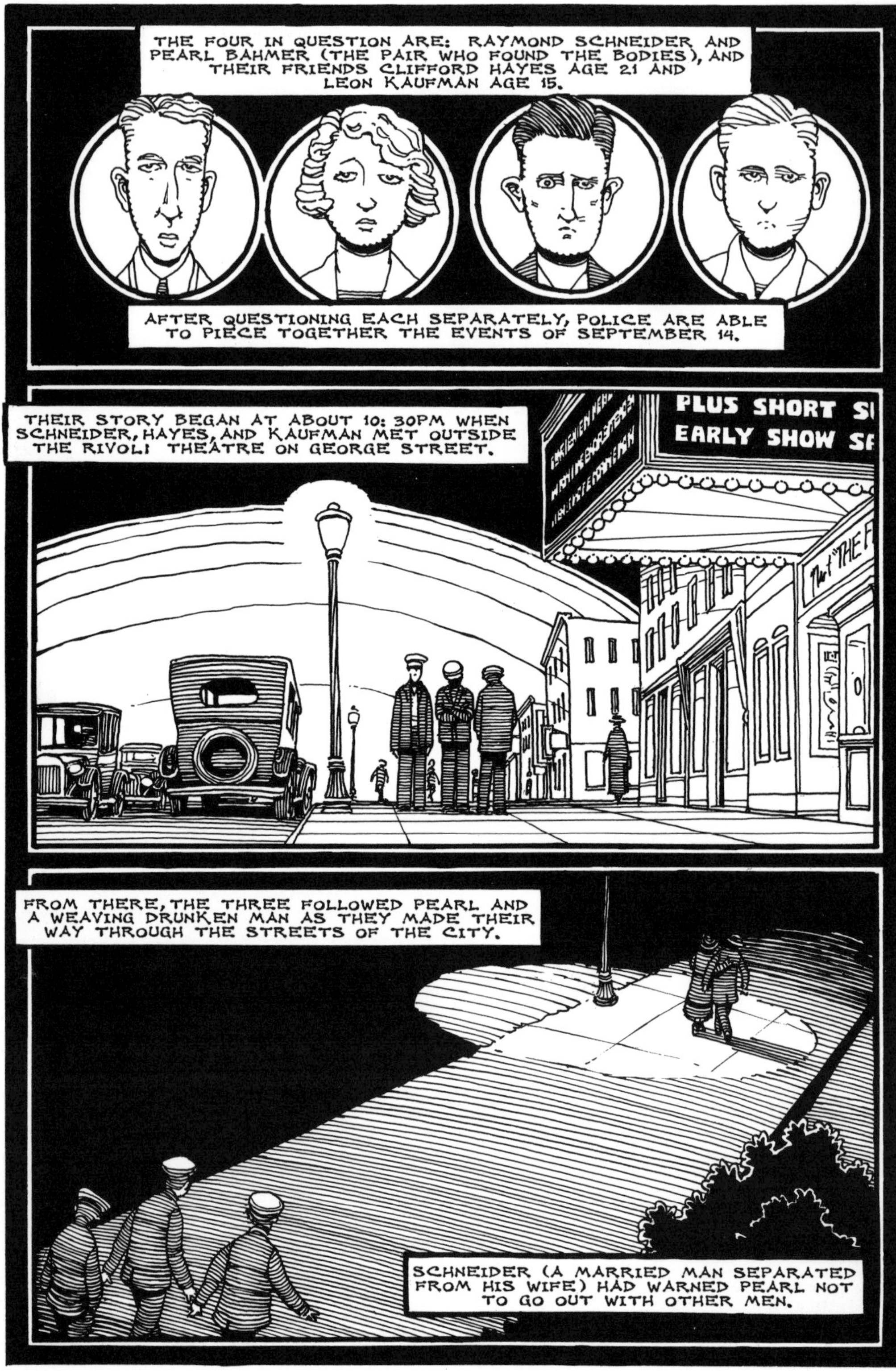
THE FOUR IN QUESTION ARE: RAYMOND SCHNEIDER AND PEARL BAHMER (THE PAIR WHO FOUND THE BODIES), AND THEIR FRIENDS CLIFFORD HAYES AGE 21 AND LEON KAUFMAN AGE 15.
AFTER QUESTIONING EACH SEPARATELY, POLICE ARE ABLE TO PIECE TOGETHER THE EVENTS OF SEPTEMBER 14.
THEIR STORY BEGAN AT ABOUT 10:30PM WHEN SCHNEIDER, HAYES, AND KAUFMAN MET OUTSIDE THE RIVOLI THEATRE ON GEORGE STREET.
PLUS SHORT
EARLY SHOW
FROM THERE, THE THREE FOLLOWED PEARL AND A WEAVING DRUNKEN MAN AS THEY MADE THEIR WAY THROUGH THE STREETS OF THE CITY.
SCHNEIDER (A MARRIED MAN SEPARATED FROM HIS WIFE) HAD WARNED PEARL NOT TO GO OUT WITH OTHER MEN.

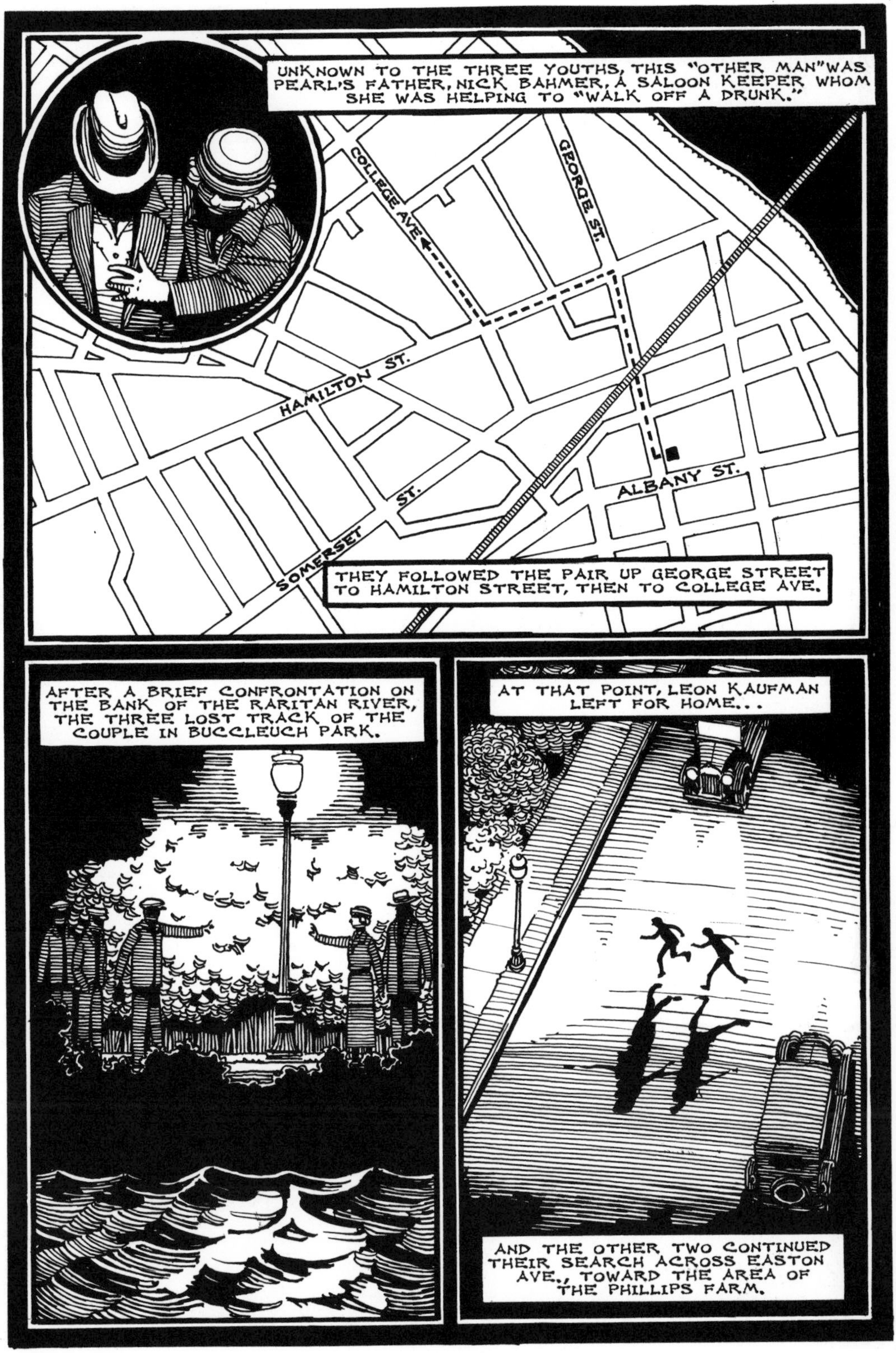
UNKNOWN TO THE THREE YOUTHS, THIS "OTHER MAN" WAS PEARL'S FATHER, NICK BAHMER, A SALOON KEEPER WHOM SHE WAS HELPING TO "WALK OFF A DRUNK."
COLLEGE AVE
GEORGE ST.
HAMILTON ST.
ALBANY ST.
SOMERSET ST.
THEY FOLLOWED THE PAIR UP GEORGE STREET TO HAMILTON STREET, THEN TO COLLEGE AVE.
AFTER A BRIEF CONFRONTATION ON THE BANK OF THE RARITAN RIVER, THE THREE LOST TRACK OF THE COUPLE IN BUCCLEUCH PARK.
AT THAT POINT, LEON KAUFMAN LEFT FOR HOME...
AND THE OTHER TWO CONTINUED THEIR SEARCH ACROSS EASTON AVE., TOWARD THE AREA OF THE PHILLIPS FARM.

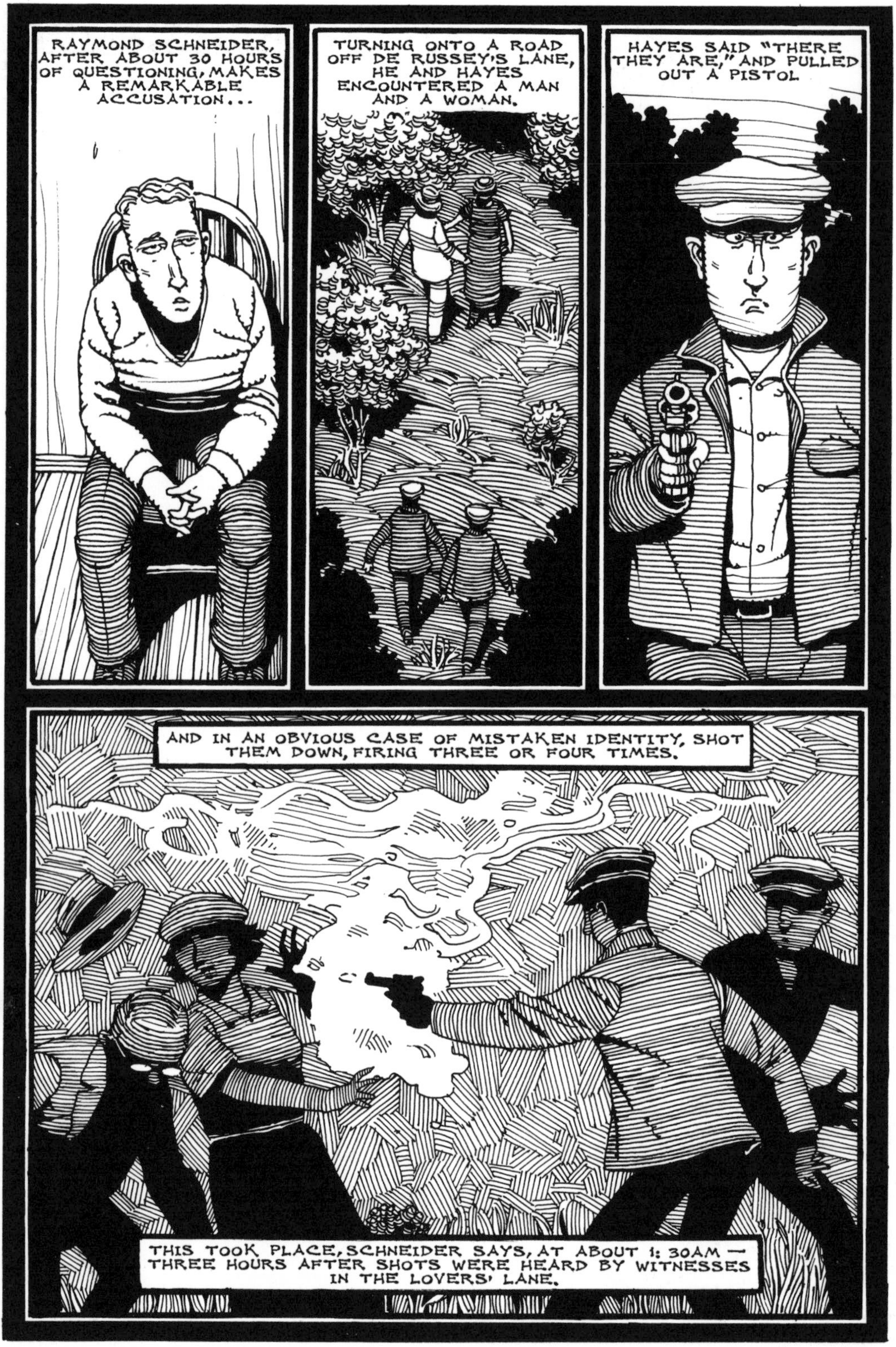
RAYMOND SCHNEIDER, AFTER ABOUT 30 HOURS OF QUESTIONING, MAKES A REMARKABLE ACCUSATION...
TURNING ONTO A ROAD OFF DE RUSSEY'S LANE, HE AND HAYES ENCOUNTERED A MAN AND A WOMAN.
HAYES SAID "THERE THEY ARE," AND PULLED OUT A PISTOL
AND IN AN OBVIOUS CASE OF MISTAKEN IDENTITY, SHOT THEM DOWN, FIRING THREE OR FOUR TIMES.
THIS TOOK PLACE, SCHNEIDER SAYS, AT ABOUT 1:30AM — THREE HOURS AFTER SHOTS WERE HEARD BY WITNESSES IN THE LOVERS' LANE.

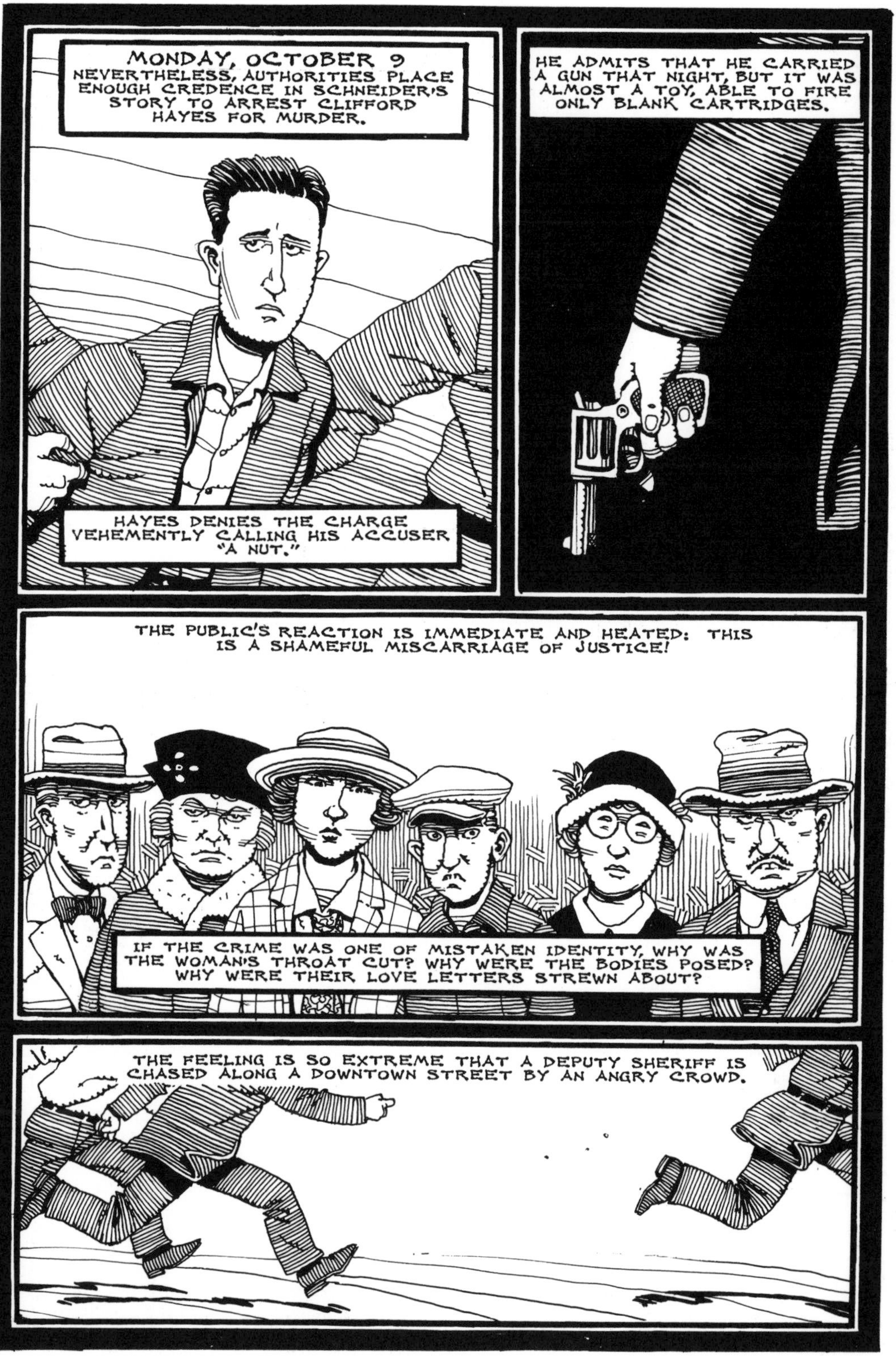
MONDAY, OCTOBER 9
NEVERTHELESS, AUTHORITIES PLACE ENOUGH CREDENCE IN SCHNEIDER'S STORY TO ARREST CLIFFORD HAYES FOR MURDER.
HAYES DENIES THE CHARGE VEHEMENTLY CALLING HIS ACCUSER "A NUT."
HE ADMITS THAT HE CARRIED A GUN THAT NIGHT, BUT IT WAS ALMOST A TOY, ABLE TO FIRE ONLY BLANK CARTRIDGES.
THE PUBLIC'S REACTION IS IMMEDIATE AND HEATED: THIS IS A SHAMEFUL MISCARRIAGE OF JUSTICE!
IF THE CRIME WAS ONE OF MISTAKEN IDENTITY, WHY WAS THE WOMAN'S THROAT CUT? WHY WERE THE BODIES POSED? WHY WERE THEIR LOVE LETTERS STREWN ABOUT?
THE FEELING IS SO EXTREME THAT A DEPUTY SHERIFF IS CHASED ALONG A DOWNTOWN STREET BY AN ANGRY CROWD.

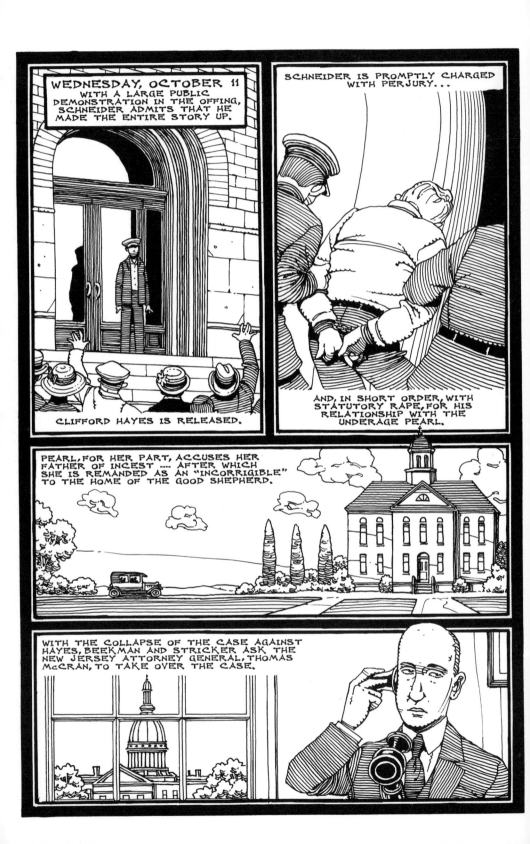

WEDNESDAY, OCTOBER 11 WITH A LARGE PUBLIC DEMONSTRATION IN THE OFFING, SCHNEIDER ADMITS THAT HE MADE THE ENTIRE STORY UP.

CLIFFORD HAYES IS RELEASED.

SCHNEIDER IS PROMPTLY CHARGED WITH PERJURY...

AND, IN SHORT ORDER, WITH STATUTORY RAPE, FOR HIS RELATIONSHIP WITH THE UNDERAGE PEARL.

PEARL, FOR HER PART, ACCUSES HER FATHER OF INCEST — AFTER WHICH SHE IS REMANDED AS AN "INCORRIGIBLE" TO THE HOME OF THE GOOD SHEPHERD.

WITH THE COLLAPSE OF THE CASE AGAINST HAYES, BEEKMAN AND STRICKER ASK THE NEW JERSEY ATTORNEY GENERAL, THOMAS McCRAN, TO TAKE OVER THE CASE.

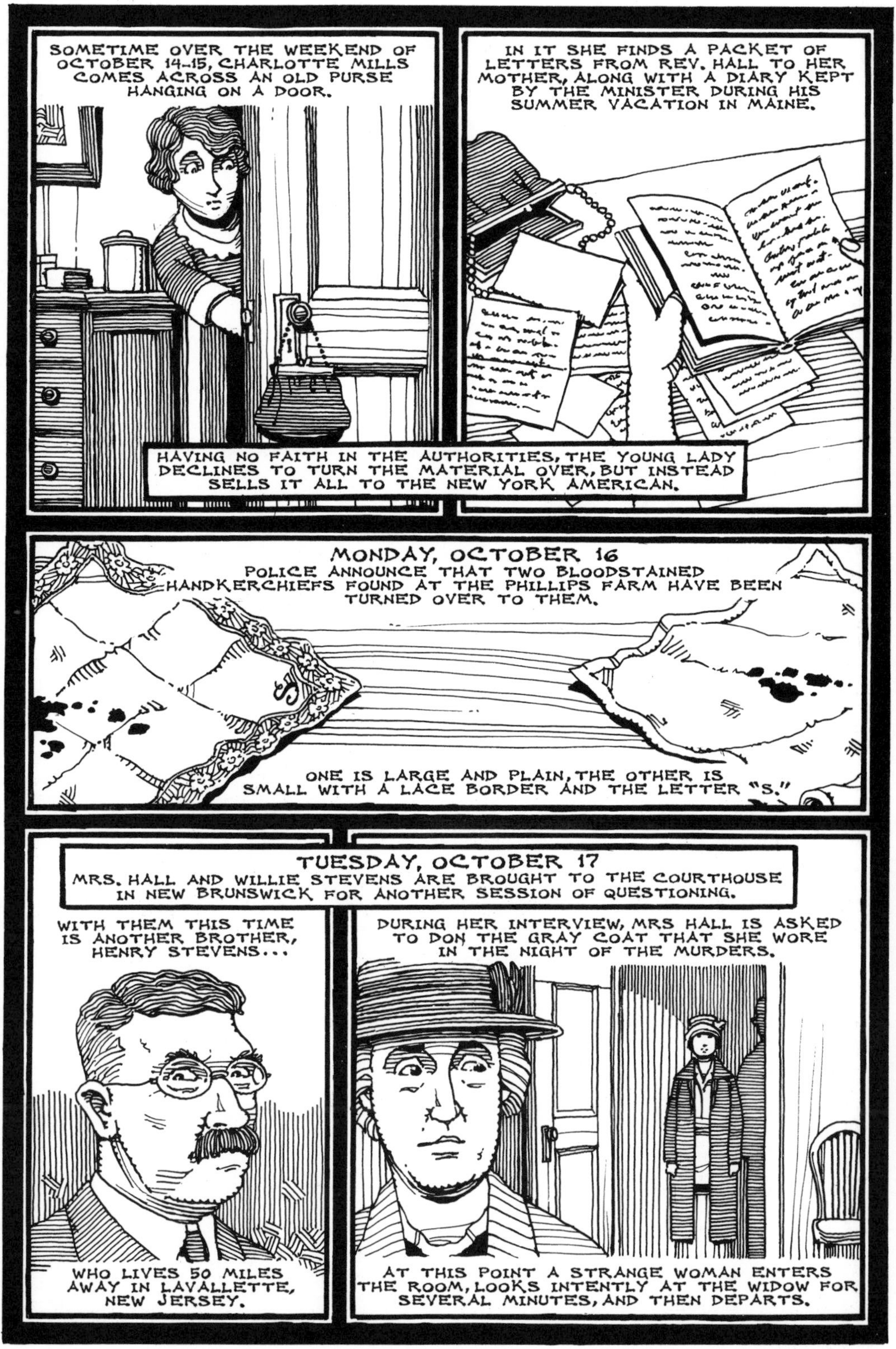
SOMETIME OVER THE WEEKEND OF OCTOBER 14-15, CHARLOTTE MILLS COMES ACROSS AN OLD PURSE HANGING ON A DOOR.
IN IT SHE FINDS A PACKET OF LETTERS FROM REV. HALL TO HER MOTHER, ALONG WITH A DIARY KEPT BY THE MINISTER DURING HIS SUMMER VACATION IN MAINE.
HAVING NO FAITH IN THE AUTHORITIES, THE YOUNG LADY DECLINES TO TURN THE MATERIAL OVER, BUT INSTEAD SELLS IT ALL TO THE NEW YORK AMERICAN.
MONDAY, OCTOBER 16
POLICE ANNOUNCE THAT TWO BLOODSTAINED HANDKERCHIEFS FOUND AT THE PHILLIPS FARM HAVE BEEN TURNED OVER TO THEM.
ONE IS LARGE AND PLAIN, THE OTHER IS SMALL WITH A LACE BORDER AND THE LETTER "S."
TUESDAY, OCTOBER 17
MRS. HALL AND WILLIE STEVENS ARE BROUGHT TO THE COURTHOUSE IN NEW BRUNSWICK FOR ANOTHER SESSION OF QUESTIONING.
WITH THEM THIS TIME IS ANOTHER BROTHER, HENRY STEVENS...
WHO LIVES 50 MILES AWAY IN LAVALLETTE, NEW JERSEY.
DURING HER INTERVIEW, MRS HALL IS ASKED TO DON THE GRAY COAT THAT SHE WORE IN THE NIGHT OF THE MURDERS.
AT THIS POINT A STRANGE WOMAN ENTERS THE ROOM, LOOKS INTENTLY AT THE WIDOW FOR SEVERAL MINUTES, AND THEN DEPARTS.

WEDNESDAY, OCTOBER 18
ON THIS DAY, DR. JOHN ANDERSON, WHO HAS EXAMINED THE SOIL WHERE THE BODIES LAY, ANNOUNCES HIS FINDINGS.

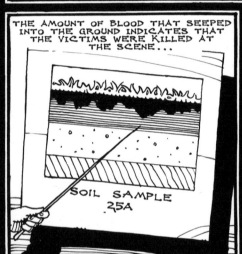

THE AMOUNT OF BLOOD THAT SEEPED INTO THE GROUND INDICATES THAT THE VICTIMS WERE KILLED AT THE SCENE...

SOIL SAMPLE 25A

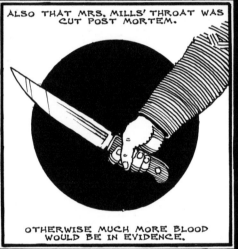

ALSO THAT MRS. MILLS' THROAT WAS CUT POST MORTEM.

OTHERWISE MUCH MORE BLOOD WOULD BE IN EVIDENCE.

THIS MEANS THAT THE CASE NOW BELONGS TO SOMERSET COUNTY AND ITS PROSECUTOR AZARIAH BEEKMAN.

HE HINTS AT A NEWLY-DISCOVERED "ANONYMOUS WITNESS," WHOSE STORY WILL SURELY SHAKE UP THE INVESTIGATION.

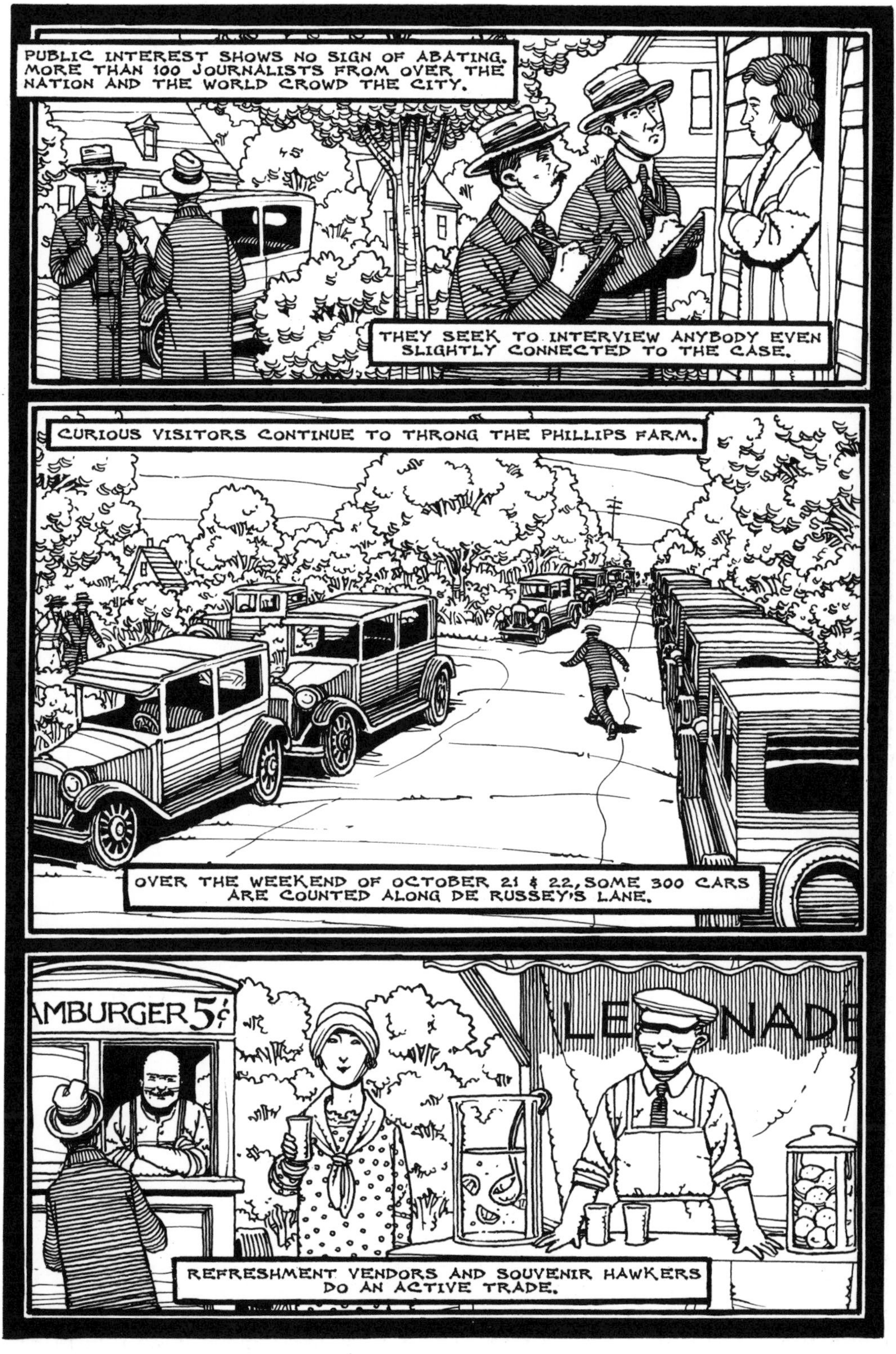
PUBLIC INTEREST SHOWS NO SIGN OF ABATING. MORE THAN 100 JOURNALISTS FROM OVER THE NATION AND THE WORLD CROWD THE CITY.
THEY SEEK TO INTERVIEW ANYBODY EVEN SLIGHTLY CONNECTED TO THE CASE.
CURIOUS VISITORS CONTINUE TO THRONG THE PHILLIPS FARM.
OVER THE WEEKEND OF OCTOBER 21 & 22, SOME 300 CARS ARE COUNTED ALONG DE RUSSEY'S LANE.
AMBURGER 5¢
LE NADE
REFRESHMENT VENDORS AND SOUVENIR HAWKERS DO AN ACTIVE TRADE.

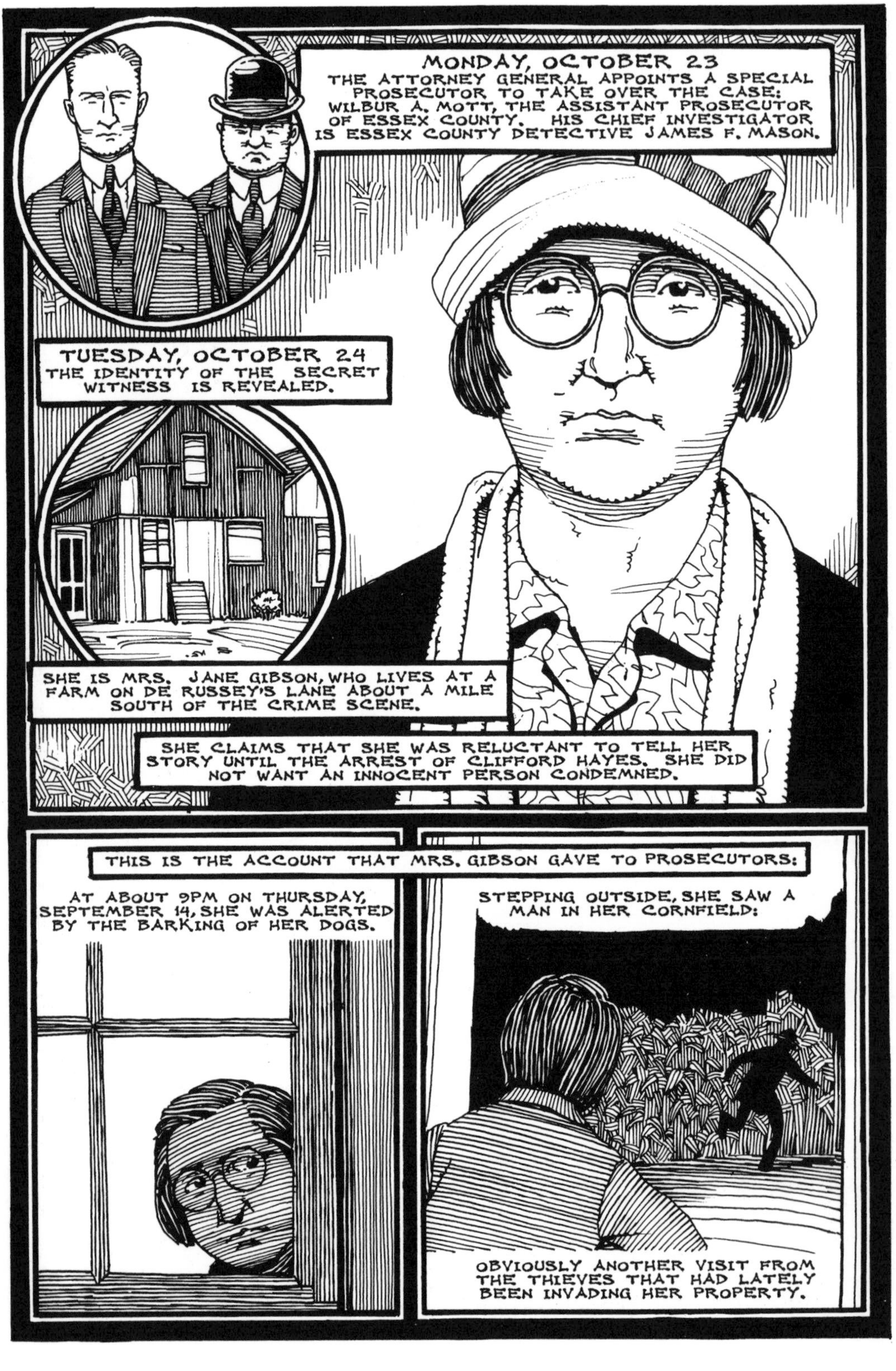
MONDAY, OCTOBER 23
THE ATTORNEY GENERAL APPOINTS A SPECIAL PROSECUTOR TO TAKE OVER THE CASE: WILBUR A. MOTT, THE ASSISTANT PROSECUTOR OF ESSEX COUNTY. HIS CHIEF INVESTIGATOR IS ESSEX COUNTY DETECTIVE JAMES F. MASON.
TUESDAY, OCTOBER 24
THE IDENTITY OF THE SECRET WITNESS IS REVEALED.
SHE IS MRS. JANE GIBSON, WHO LIVES AT A FARM ON DE RUSSEY'S LANE ABOUT A MILE SOUTH OF THE CRIME SCENE.
SHE CLAIMS THAT SHE WAS RELUCTANT TO TELL HER STORY UNTIL THE ARREST OF CLIFFORD HAYES. SHE DID NOT WANT AN INNOCENT PERSON CONDEMNED.
THIS IS THE ACCOUNT THAT MRS. GIBSON GAVE TO PROSECUTORS:
AT ABOUT 9PM ON THURSDAY, SEPTEMBER 14, SHE WAS ALERTED BY THE BARKING OF HER DOGS.
STEPPING OUTSIDE, SHE SAW A MAN IN HER CORNFIELD:
OBVIOUSLY ANOTHER VISIT FROM THE THIEVES THAT HAD LATELY BEEN INVADING HER PROPERTY.

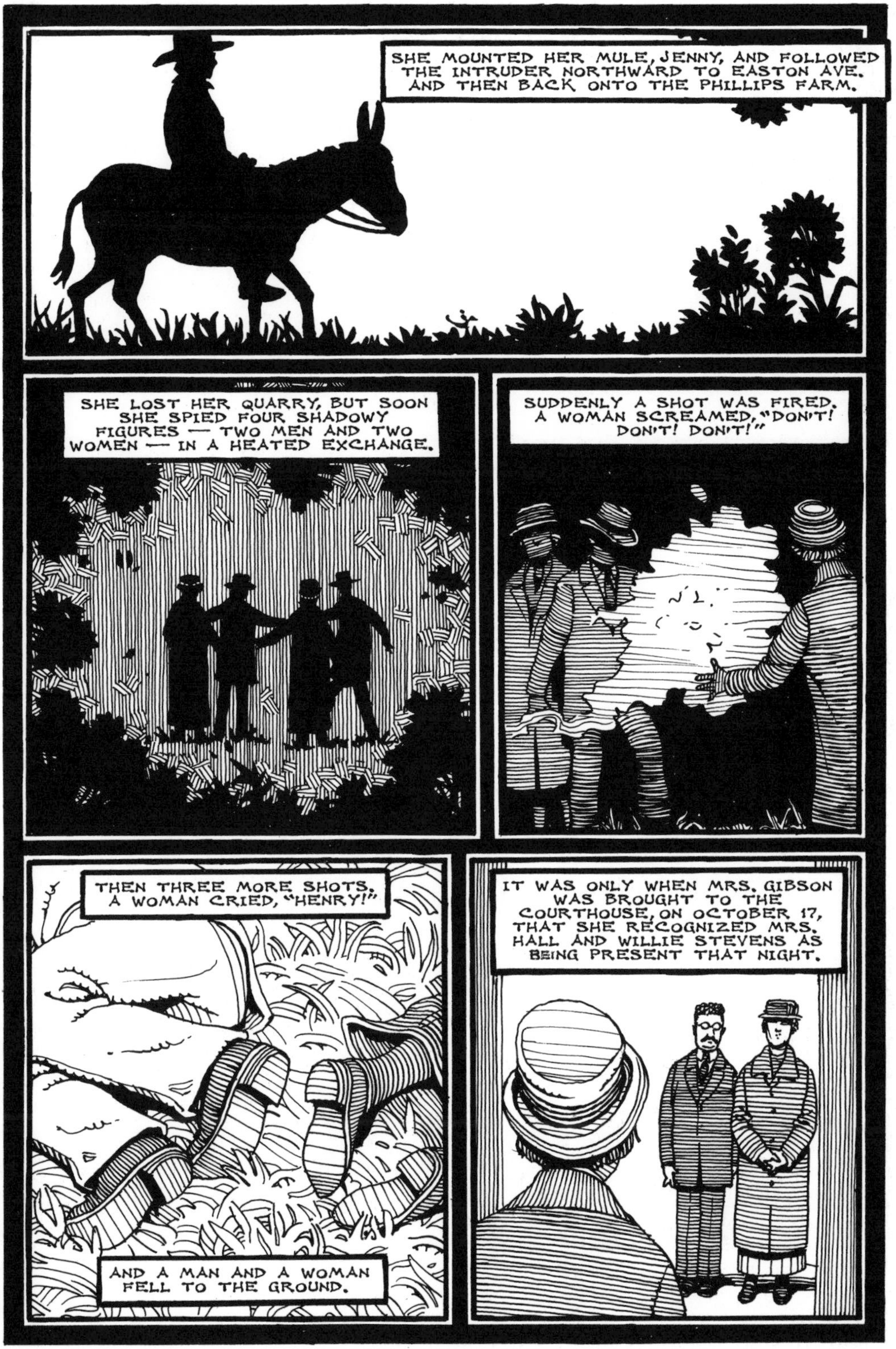
SHE MOUNTED HER MULE, JENNY, AND FOLLOWED THE INTRUDER NORTHWARD TO EASTON AVE. AND THEN BACK ONTO THE PHILLIPS FARM.
SHE LOST HER QUARRY, BUT SOON SHE SPIED FOUR SHADOWY FIGURES — TWO MEN AND TWO WOMEN — IN A HEATED EXCHANGE.
SUDDENLY A SHOT WAS FIRED. A WOMAN SCREAMED, "DON'T! DON'T! DON'T!"
THEN THREE MORE SHOTS. A WOMAN CRIED, "HENRY!"
AND A MAN AND A WOMAN FELL TO THE GROUND.
IT WAS ONLY WHEN MRS. GIBSON WAS BROUGHT TO THE COURTHOUSE, ON OCTOBER 17, THAT SHE RECOGNIZED MRS. HALL AND WILLIE STEVENS AS BEING PRESENT THAT NIGHT.

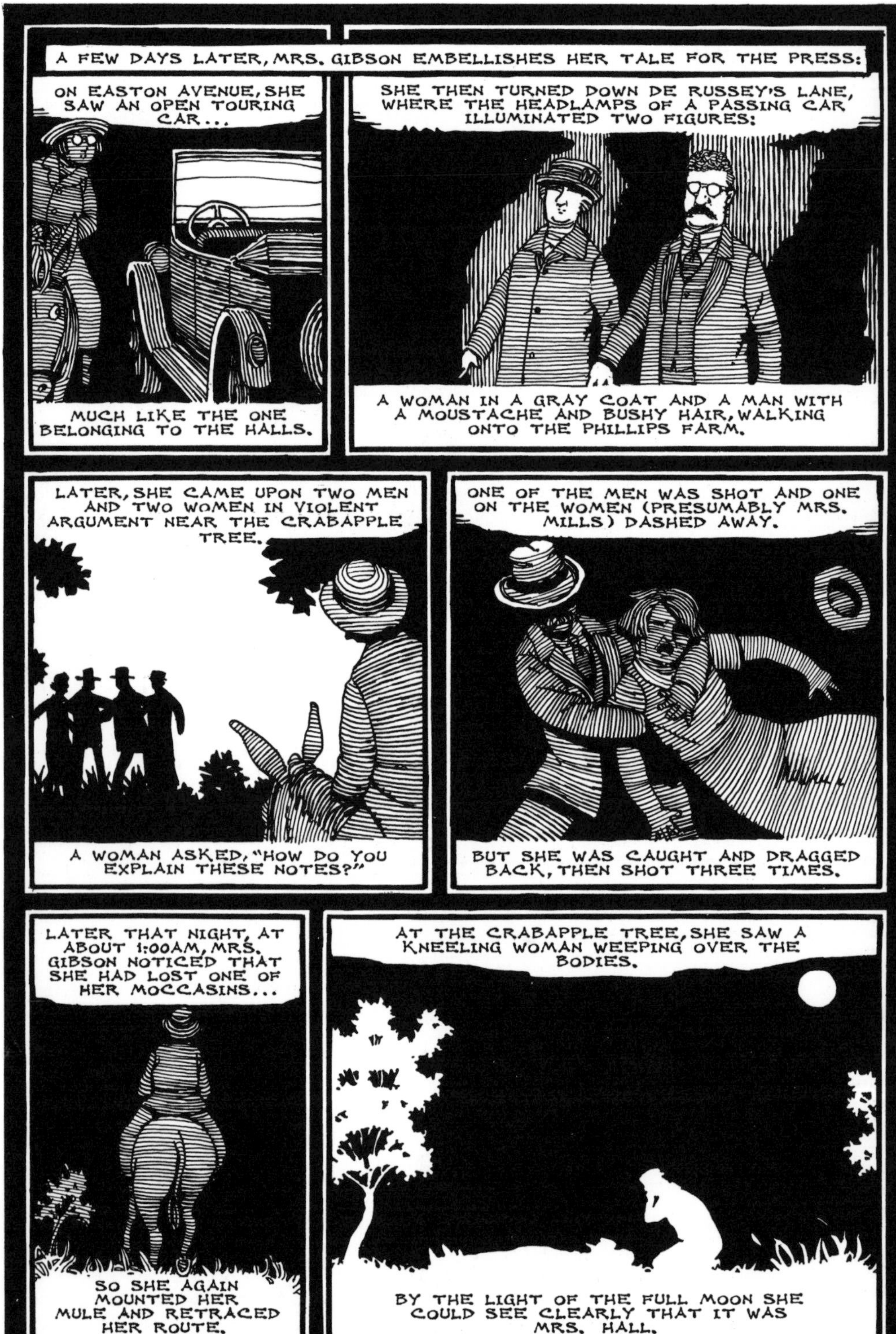
A FEW DAYS LATER, MRS. GIBSON EMBELLISHES HER TALE FOR THE PRESS:
ON EASTON AVENUE, SHE SAW AN OPEN TOURING CAR...
MUCH LIKE THE ONE BELONGING TO THE HALLS.
SHE THEN TURNED DOWN DE RUSSEY'S LANE, WHERE THE HEADLAMPS OF A PASSING CAR ILLUMINATED TWO FIGURES:
A WOMAN IN A GRAY COAT AND A MAN WITH A MOUSTACHE AND BUSHY HAIR, WALKING ONTO THE PHILLIPS FARM.
LATER, SHE CAME UPON TWO MEN AND TWO WOMEN IN VIOLENT ARGUMENT NEAR THE CRABAPPLE TREE.
A WOMAN ASKED, "HOW DO YOU EXPLAIN THESE NOTES?"
ONE OF THE MEN WAS SHOT AND ONE ON THE WOMEN (PRESUMABLY MRS. MILLS) DASHED AWAY.
BUT SHE WAS CAUGHT AND DRAGGED BACK, THEN SHOT THREE TIMES.
LATER THAT NIGHT, AT ABOUT 1:00AM, MRS. GIBSON NOTICED THAT SHE HAD LOST ONE OF HER MOCCASINS...
SO SHE AGAIN MOUNTED HER MULE AND RETRACED HER ROUTE.
AT THE CRABAPPLE TREE, SHE SAW A KNEELING WOMAN WEEPING OVER THE BODIES.
BY THE LIGHT OF THE FULL MOON SHE COULD SEE CLEARLY THAT IT WAS MRS. HALL.

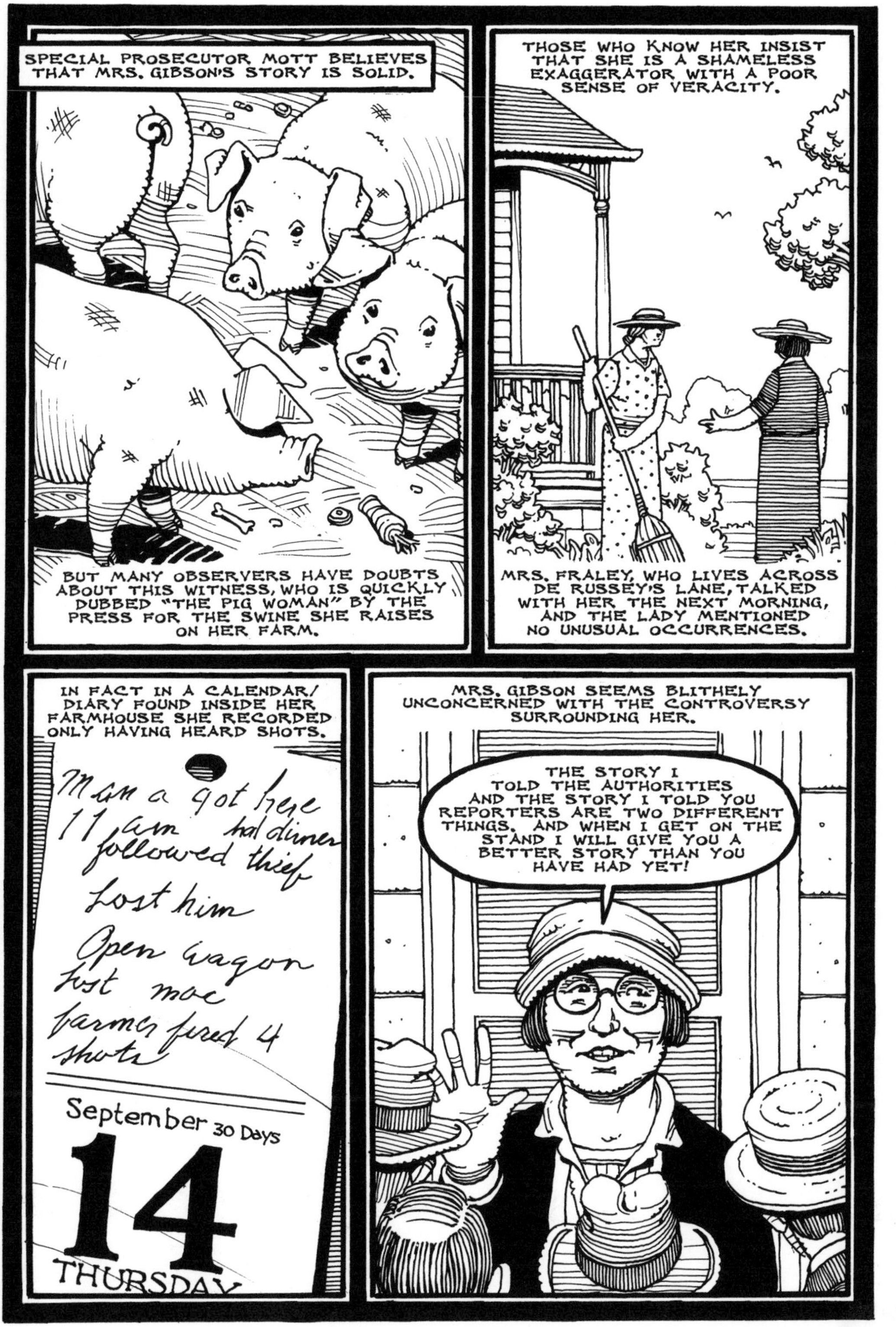

SPECIAL PROSECUTOR MOTT BELIEVES THAT MRS. GIBSON'S STORY IS SOLID.
BUT MANY OBSERVERS HAVE DOUBTS ABOUT THIS WITNESS, WHO IS QUICKLY DUBBED "THE PIG WOMAN" BY THE PRESS FOR THE SWINE SHE RAISES ON HER FARM.
THOSE WHO KNOW HER INSIST THAT SHE IS A SHAMELESS EXAGGERATOR WITH A POOR SENSE OF VERACITY.
MRS. FRALEY, WHO LIVES ACROSS DE RUSSEY'S LANE, TALKED WITH HER THE NEXT MORNING, AND THE LADY MENTIONED NO UNUSUAL OCCURRENCES.
IN FACT IN A CALENDAR/DIARY FOUND INSIDE HER FARMHOUSE SHE RECORDED ONLY HAVING HEARD SHOTS.
Man a got here
11 am had dinner
followed thief
Lost him
Open wagon
lost moc
farmer fired 4
shots
September 30 Days
14
THURSDAY
MRS. GIBSON SEEMS BLITHELY UNCONCERNED WITH THE CONTROVERSY SURROUNDING HER.
THE STORY I TOLD THE AUTHORITIES AND THE STORY I TOLD YOU REPORTERS ARE TWO DIFFERENT THINGS. AND WHEN I GET ON THE STAND I WILL GIVE YOU A BETTER STORY THAN YOU HAVE HAD YET!

ONE INTRIGUING ELEMENT OF MRS. GIBSON'S ACCOUNT HAS A WOMAN CRY OUT THE NAME:

HENRY!

WHO IS "HENRY?" THERE ARE TWO OBVIOUS CANDIDATES.

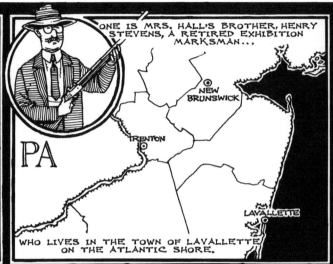

ONE IS MRS. HALL'S BROTHER, HENRY STEVENS, A RETIRED EXHIBITION MARKSMAN...

PA

NEW BRUNSWICK

TRENTON

LAVALLETTE

WHO LIVES IN THE TOWN OF LAVALLETTE ON THE ATLANTIC SHORE.

BUT HE HAS BEEN ESTRANGED FROM HIS SISTER FOR MANY YEARS...

AND, MOREOVER, WAS SEEN FISHING BY SEVERAL NEIGHBORS ON THE EVENING IN QUESTION.

THE OTHER POSSIBILITY IS HENRY CARPENDER A STOCKBROKER AND A COUSIN OF MRS. HALL...

WHO LIVES NEAR THE HALLS ON NICHOL AVE.

HIS ALIBI ALSO APPEARS UNSHAKABLE.

HE AND HIS WIFE HAD DINNER WITH FRIENDS UNTIL 10:30PM ON THE FATEFUL THURSDAY NIGHT.

NEVERTHELESS, HE IS RECOGNIZED BY MRS. GIBSON WHEN SHE IS BROUGHT TO THE PENNSYLVANIA DEPOT TO PICK HIM OUT OF THE CROWD.

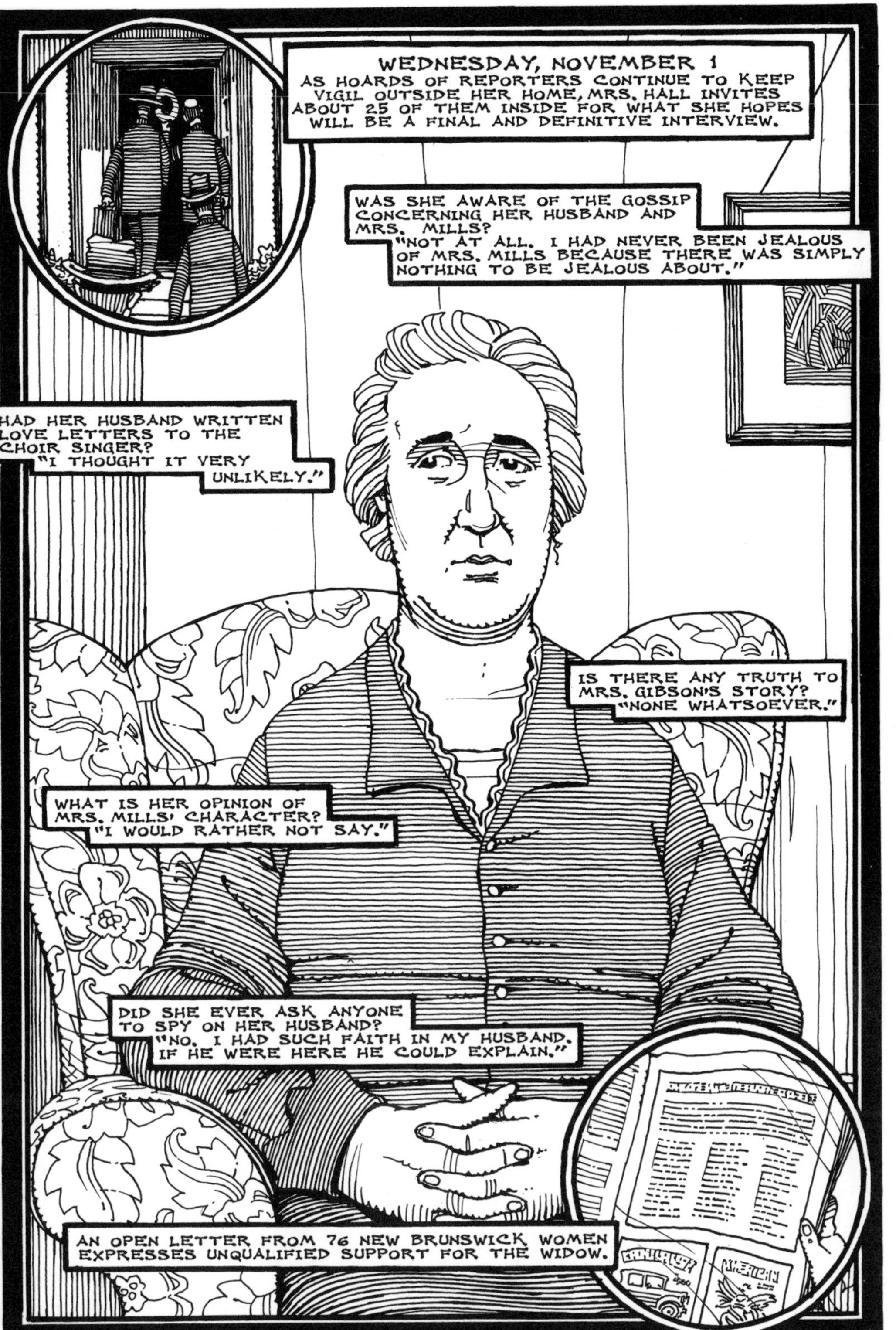
WEDNESDAY, NOVEMBER 1
AS HOARDS OF REPORTERS CONTINUE TO KEEP VIGIL OUTSIDE HER HOME, MRS. HALL INVITES ABOUT 25 OF THEM INSIDE FOR WHAT SHE HOPES WILL BE A FINAL AND DEFINITIVE INTERVIEW.
WAS SHE AWARE OF THE GOSSIP CONCERNING HER HUSBAND AND MRS. MILLS?
"NOT AT ALL. I HAD NEVER BEEN JEALOUS OF MRS. MILLS BECAUSE THERE WAS SIMPLY NOTHING TO BE JEALOUS ABOUT."
HAD HER HUSBAND WRITTEN LOVE LETTERS TO THE CHOIR SINGER?
"I THOUGHT IT VERY UNLIKELY."
IS THERE ANY TRUTH TO MRS. GIBSON'S STORY?
"NONE WHATSOEVER."
WHAT IS HER OPINION OF MRS. MILLS' CHARACTER?
"I WOULD RATHER NOT SAY."
DID SHE EVER ASK ANYONE TO SPY ON HER HUSBAND?
"NO. I HAD SUCH FAITH IN MY HUSBAND. IF HE WERE HERE HE COULD EXPLAIN."
AN OPEN LETTER FROM 76 NEW BRUNSWICK WOMEN EXPRESSES UNQUALIFIED SUPPORT FOR THE WIDOW.

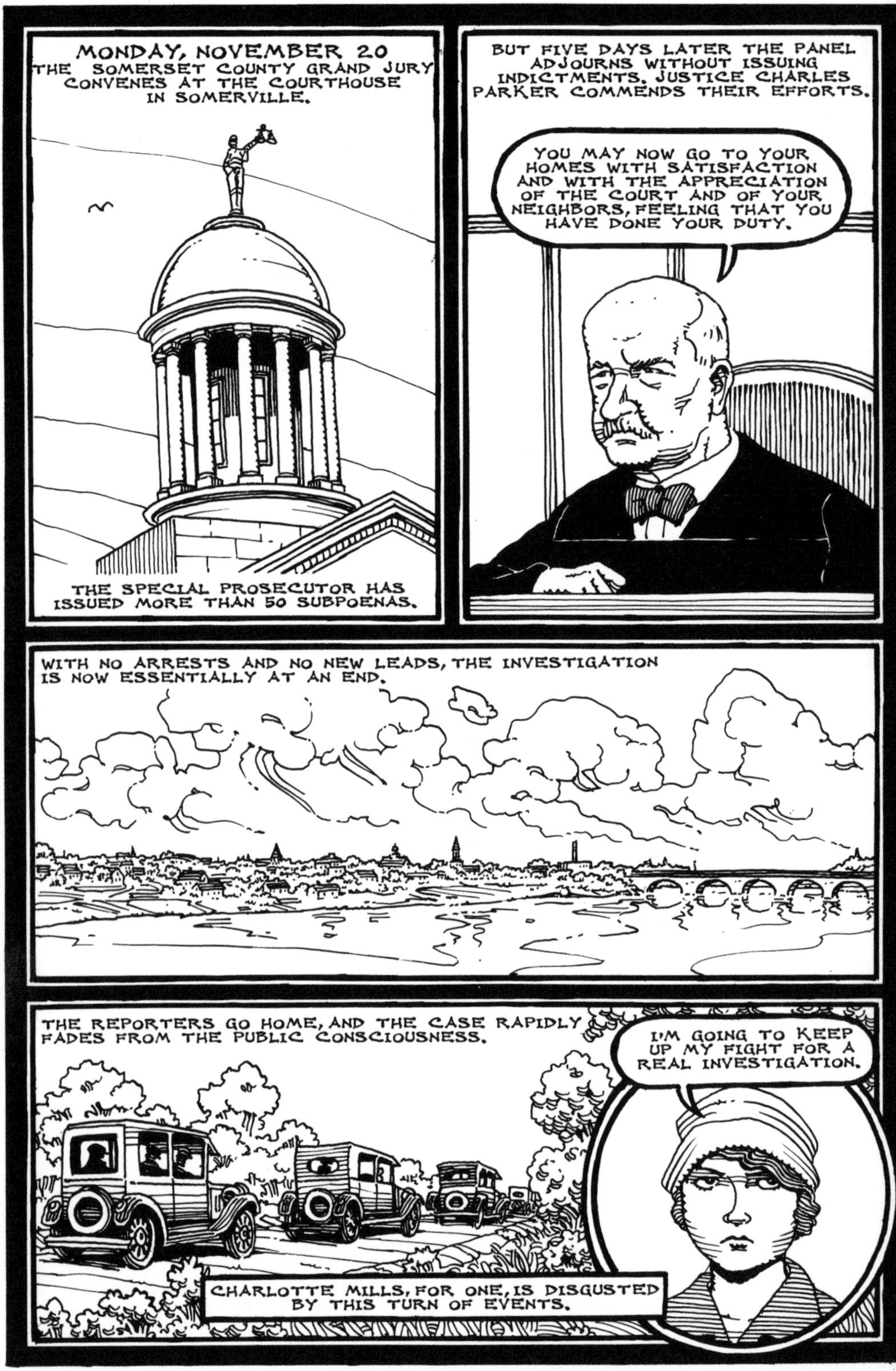
MONDAY, NOVEMBER 20
THE SOMERSET COUNTY GRAND JURY CONVENES AT THE COURTHOUSE IN SOMERVILLE.
THE SPECIAL PROSECUTOR HAS ISSUED MORE THAN 50 SUBPOENAS.
BUT FIVE DAYS LATER THE PANEL ADJOURNS WITHOUT ISSUING INDICTMENTS. JUSTICE CHARLES PARKER COMMENDS THEIR EFFORTS.
YOU MAY NOW GO TO YOUR HOMES WITH SATISFACTION AND WITH THE APPRECIATION OF THE COURT AND OF YOUR NEIGHBORS, FEELING THAT YOU HAVE DONE YOUR DUTY.
WITH NO ARRESTS AND NO NEW LEADS, THE INVESTIGATION IS NOW ESSENTIALLY AT AN END.
THE REPORTERS GO HOME, AND THE CASE RAPIDLY FADES FROM THE PUBLIC CONSCIOUSNESS.
I'M GOING TO KEEP UP MY FIGHT FOR A REAL INVESTIGATION.
CHARLOTTE MILLS, FOR ONE, IS DISGUSTED BY THIS TURN OF EVENTS.

PART V

FOUR YEARS LATER

FOR THE NEXT FOUR YEARS, THE HALL-MILLS MURDER CASE LIES FORGOTTEN IN THE FILES OF THE SOMERSET AND MIDDLESEX COUNTIES...

ALTHOUGH OFFICIALS CONTINUE TO HOLD OUT HOPE FOR AN EVENTUAL SOLUTION AND HINT PERIODICALLY AT AN IMPENDING BREAKTHROUGH.

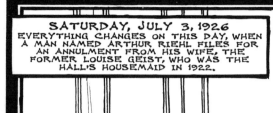
SATURDAY, JULY 3, 1926
EVERYTHING CHANGES ON THIS DAY, WHEN A MAN NAMED ARTHUR RIEHL FILES FOR AN ANNULMENT FROM HIS WIFE, THE FORMER LOUISE GEIST, WHO WAS THE HALL'S HOUSEMAID IN 1922.

HE CHARGES THAT HIS WIFE HAS WITHHELD CRUCIAL INFORMATION ABOUT THE MURDERS.

SHE HAD DISCOVERED, HE CLAIMS, THAT REV. HALL AND MRS. MILLS INTENDED TO ELOPE ON THE NIGHT OF ON SEPTEMBER 14, 1922

AND PASSED THIS INFORMATION TO THE LADY OF THE HOUSE.

MRS. HALL AND WILLIE WERE DRIVEN BY PETER TUMULTY, THE FAMILY'S CHAUFFEUR AND HANDYMAN, TO DE RUSSEY'S LANE AND THE PHILLIPS FARM...

INTENDING ONLY TO CONFRONT THE ILLICIT LOVERS...

BUT ENDED UP KILLING THEM INSTEAD.

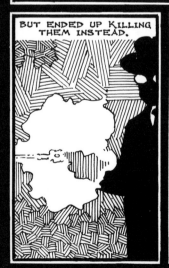

FOR HER SILENCE THE MAID RECEIVED $5000.

LOUISE, FOR HER PART, DECLARES IT ALL:

A PACK OF LIES!

BUT THE CASE IS ONCE AGAIN ON EVERYONE'S LIPS.

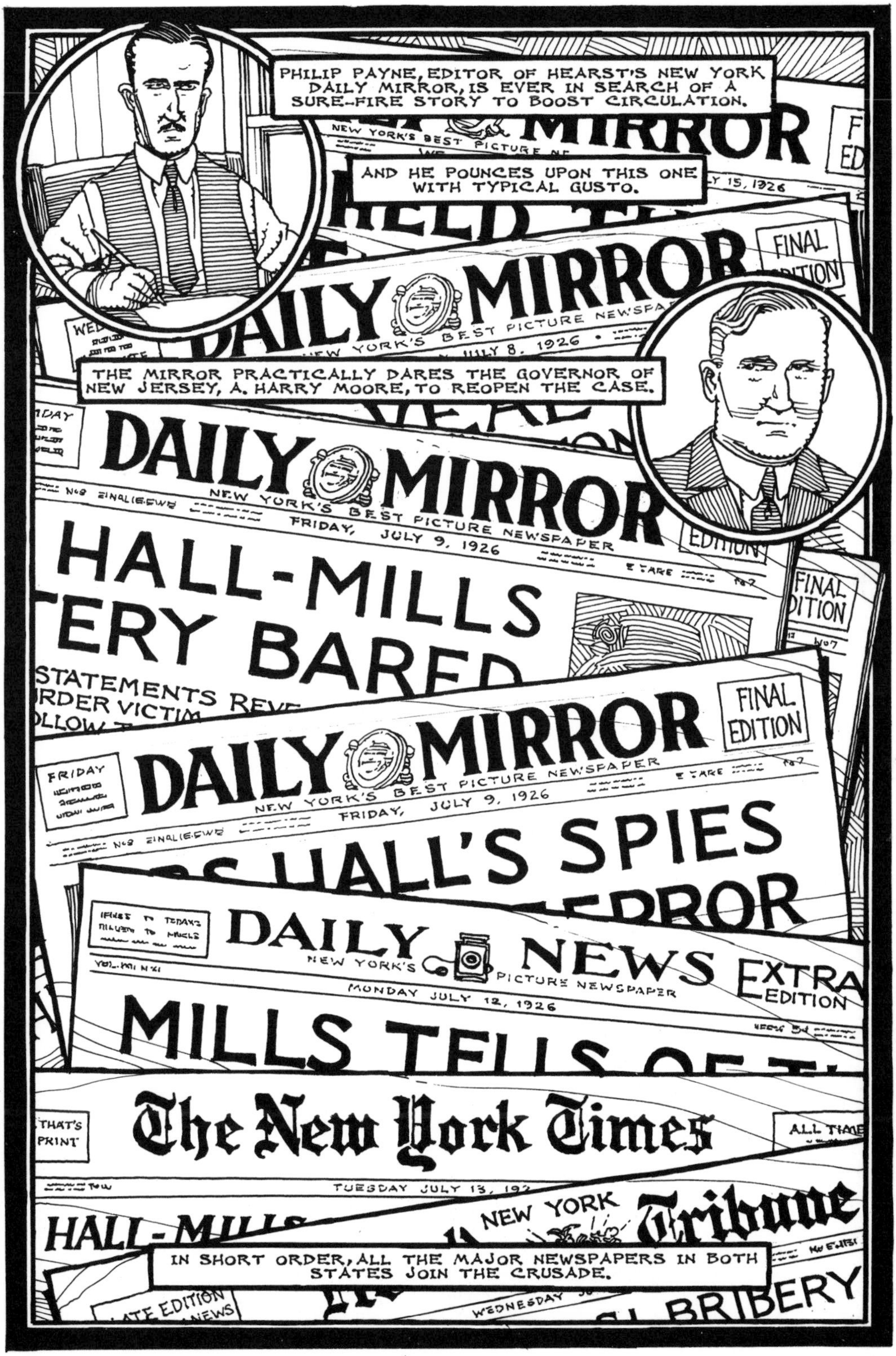
PHILIP PAYNE, EDITOR OF HEARST'S NEW YORK DAILY MIRROR, IS EVER IN SEARCH OF A SURE-FIRE STORY TO BOOST CIRCULATION.
MIRROR
NEW YORK'S BEST PICTURE
AND HE POUNCES UPON THIS ONE WITH TYPICAL GUSTO.
JULY 15, 1926
DAILY MIRROR
NEW YORK'S BEST PICTURE NEWSPAPER
JULY 8, 1926
FINAL EDITION
THE MIRROR PRACTICALLY DARES THE GOVERNOR OF NEW JERSEY, A. HARRY MOORE, TO REOPEN THE CASE.
DAILY MIRROR
NEW YORK'S BEST PICTURE NEWSPAPER
FRIDAY, JULY 9, 1926
HALL-MILLS
TERY BARED
STATEMENTS REVE
RDER VICTIM
FINAL EDITION
DAILY MIRROR
NEW YORK'S BEST PICTURE NEWSPAPER
FRIDAY, JULY 9, 1926
FINAL EDITION
FRIDAY
HALL'S SPIES
RROR
DAILY NEWS
NEW YORK'S PICTURE NEWSPAPER
MONDAY JULY 12, 1926
EXTRA EDITION
MILLS TELLS
The New York Times
THAT'S PRINT
ALL TIME
TUESDAY JULY 13, 192
HALL-MILL
NEW YORK Tribune
IN SHORT ORDER, ALL THE MAJOR NEWSPAPERS IN BOTH STATES JOIN THE CRUSADE.
LATE EDITION
NEWS
WEDNESDAY
BRIBERY

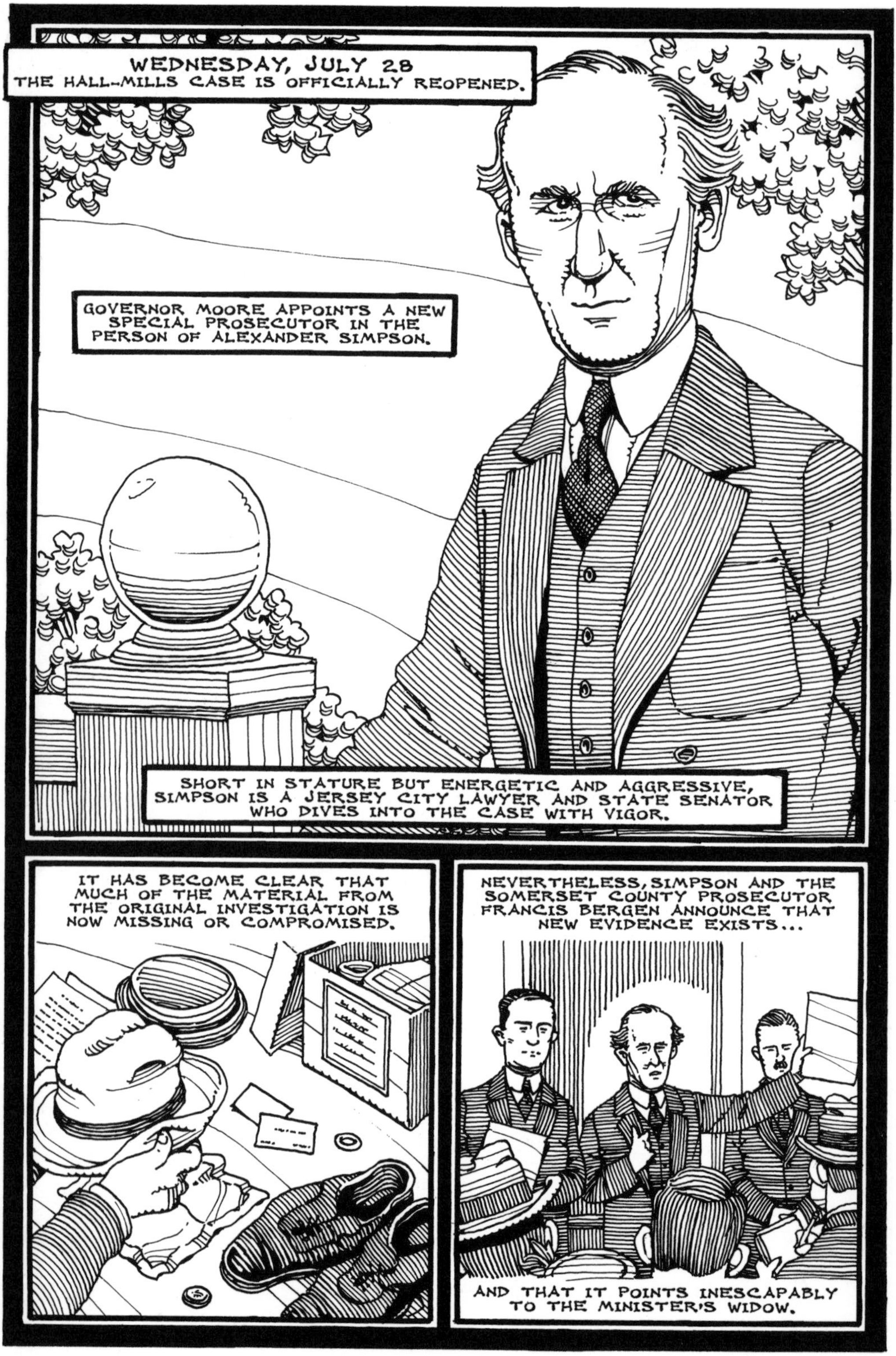
WEDNESDAY, JULY 28
THE HALL-MILLS CASE IS OFFICIALLY REOPENED.
GOVERNOR MOORE APPOINTS A NEW SPECIAL PROSECUTOR IN THE PERSON OF ALEXANDER SIMPSON.
SHORT IN STATURE BUT ENERGETIC AND AGGRESSIVE, SIMPSON IS A JERSEY CITY LAWYER AND STATE SENATOR WHO DIVES INTO THE CASE WITH VIGOR.
IT HAS BECOME CLEAR THAT MUCH OF THE MATERIAL FROM THE ORIGINAL INVESTIGATION IS NOW MISSING OR COMPROMISED.
NEVERTHELESS, SIMPSON AND THE SOMERSET COUNTY PROSECUTOR FRANCIS BERGEN ANNOUNCE THAT NEW EVIDENCE EXISTS...
AND THAT IT POINTS INESCAPABLY TO THE MINISTER'S WIDOW.

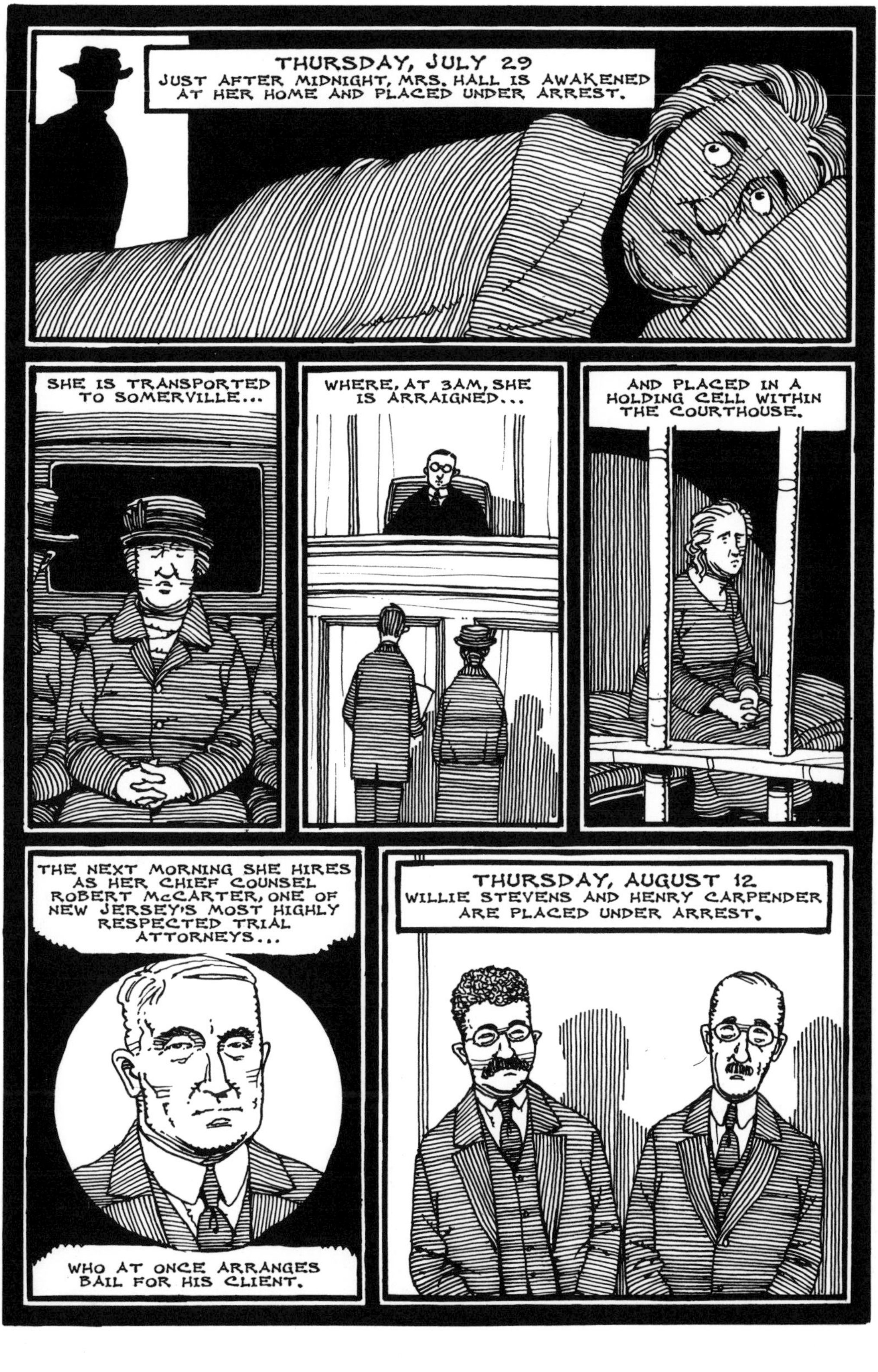
THURSDAY, JULY 29
JUST AFTER MIDNIGHT, MRS. HALL IS AWAKENED AT HER HOME AND PLACED UNDER ARREST.
SHE IS TRANSPORTED TO SOMERVILLE...
WHERE, AT 3AM, SHE IS ARRAIGNED...
AND PLACED IN A HOLDING CELL WITHIN THE COURTHOUSE.
THE NEXT MORNING SHE HIRES AS HER CHIEF COUNSEL ROBERT McCARTER, ONE OF NEW JERSEY'S MOST HIGHLY RESPECTED TRIAL ATTORNEYS...
WHO AT ONCE ARRANGES BAIL FOR HIS CLIENT.
THURSDAY, AUGUST 12
WILLIE STEVENS AND HENRY CARPENDER ARE PLACED UNDER ARREST.

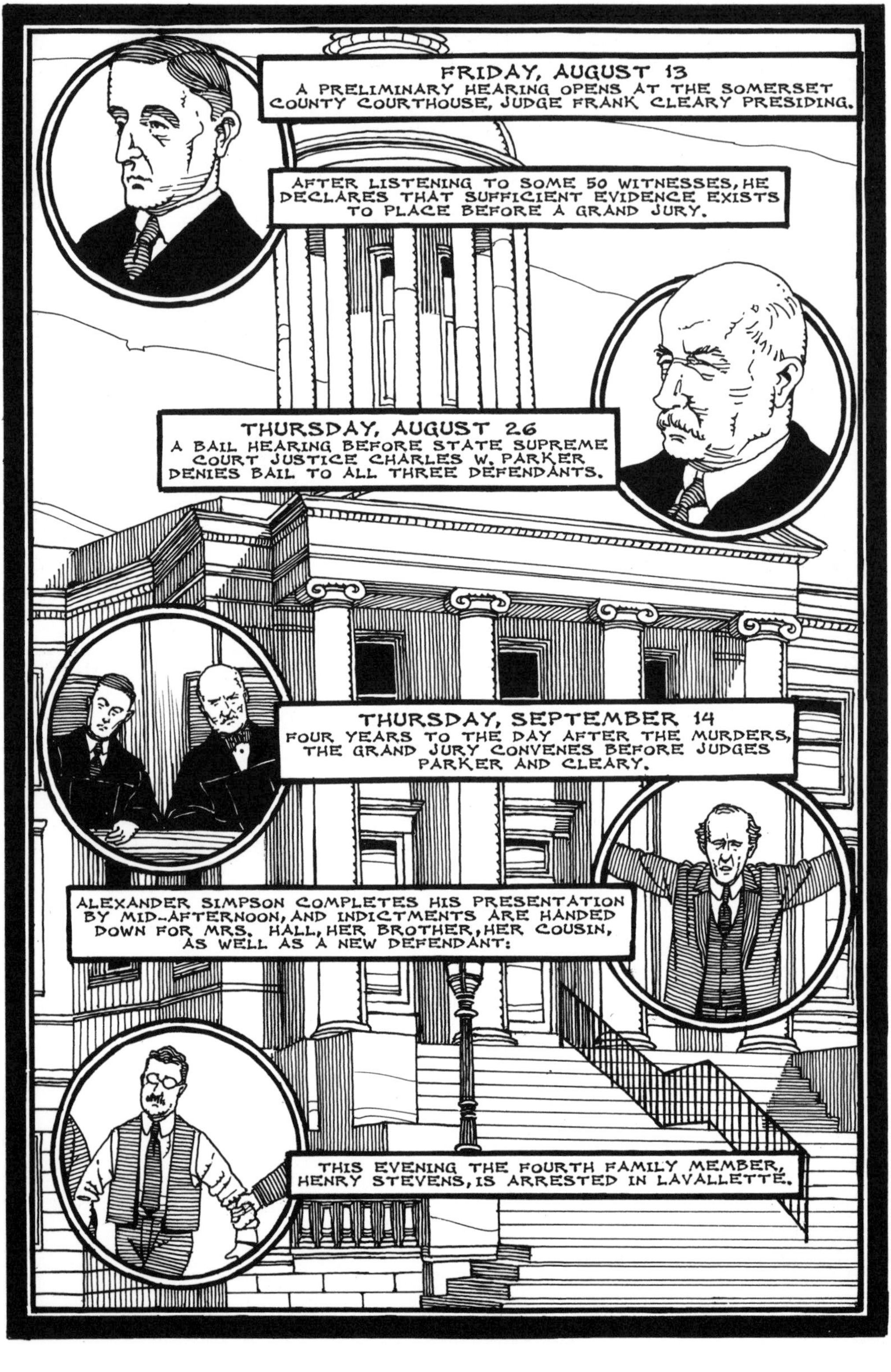
FRIDAY, AUGUST 13
A PRELIMINARY HEARING OPENS AT THE SOMERSET COUNTY COURTHOUSE, JUDGE FRANK CLEARY PRESIDING.
AFTER LISTENING TO SOME 50 WITNESSES, HE DECLARES THAT SUFFICIENT EVIDENCE EXISTS TO PLACE BEFORE A GRAND JURY.
THURSDAY, AUGUST 26
A BAIL HEARING BEFORE STATE SUPREME COURT JUSTICE CHARLES W. PARKER DENIES BAIL TO ALL THREE DEFENDANTS.
THURSDAY, SEPTEMBER 14
FOUR YEARS TO THE DAY AFTER THE MURDERS, THE GRAND JURY CONVENES BEFORE JUDGES PARKER AND CLEARY.
ALEXANDER SIMPSON COMPLETES HIS PRESENTATION BY MID-AFTERNOON, AND INDICTMENTS ARE HANDED DOWN FOR MRS. HALL, HER BROTHER, HER COUSIN, AS WELL AS A NEW DEFENDANT:
THIS EVENING THE FOURTH FAMILY MEMBER, HENRY STEVENS, IS ARRESTED IN LAVALLETTE.

FRIDAY, SEPTEMBER 17
THE FOUR ARE ARRAIGNED AND PLEAD:

NOT GUILTY.

MRS. HALL IS GRANTED BAIL OF $40,000...

WHILE THE OTHERS REMAIN BEHIND BARS.

TUESDAY, SEPTEMBER 21
THE CASE OF HENRY CARPENDER IS SEPARATED FROM THE OTHERS, SINCE HE IS CONSIDERED AN ACCESSORY AFTER THE FACT.

HIS TRIAL WILL BE CONDUCTED AT A LATER DATE.

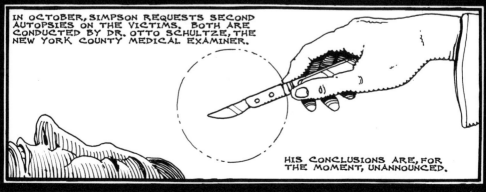
IN OCTOBER, SIMPSON REQUESTS SECOND AUTOPSIES ON THE VICTIMS. BOTH ARE CONDUCTED BY DR. OTTO SCHULTZE, THE NEW YORK COUNTY MEDICAL EXAMINER.

HIS CONCLUSIONS ARE, FOR THE MOMENT, UNANNOUNCED.

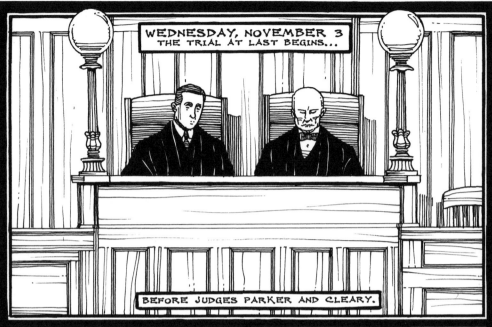

WEDNESDAY, NOVEMBER 3
THE TRIAL AT LAST BEGINS...

BEFORE JUDGES PARKER AND CLEARY.

THE PROSECUTION: HEADED BY ALEXANDER SIMPSON, ASSISTED BY FRANCIS BERGEN.

THE HALL-STEVENS "MILLION-DOLLAR DEFENSE" NOW INCLUDES, IN ADDITION TO ROBERT McCARTER, STATE SENATOR CLARENCE E. CASE.

A JURY, TO THE SURPRISE OF ALL, IS CHOSEN IN LESS THAN AN HOUR.

IT CONSISTS ENTIRELY OF OLDER MARRIED MEN.

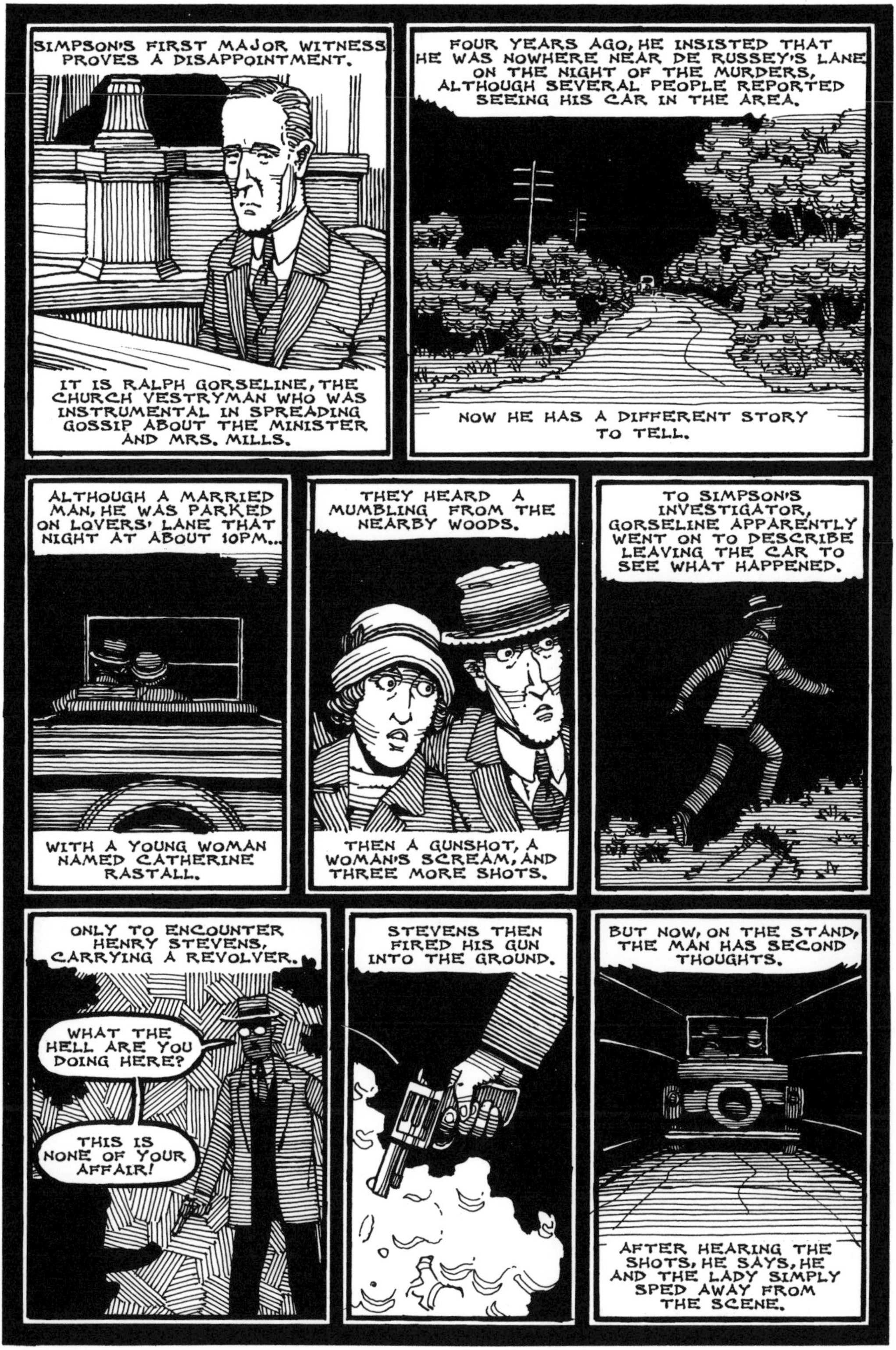
SIMPSON'S FIRST MAJOR WITNESS PROVES A DISAPPOINTMENT.
IT IS RALPH GORSELINE, THE CHURCH VESTRYMAN WHO WAS INSTRUMENTAL IN SPREADING GOSSIP ABOUT THE MINISTER AND MRS. MILLS.
FOUR YEARS AGO, HE INSISTED THAT HE WAS NOWHERE NEAR DE RUSSEY'S LANE ON THE NIGHT OF THE MURDERS, ALTHOUGH SEVERAL PEOPLE REPORTED SEEING HIS CAR IN THE AREA.
NOW HE HAS A DIFFERENT STORY TO TELL.
ALTHOUGH A MARRIED MAN, HE WAS PARKED ON LOVERS' LANE THAT NIGHT AT ABOUT 10PM...
WITH A YOUNG WOMAN NAMED CATHERINE RASTALL.
THEY HEARD A MUMBLING FROM THE NEARBY WOODS.
THEN A GUNSHOT, A WOMAN'S SCREAM, AND THREE MORE SHOTS.
TO SIMPSON'S INVESTIGATOR, GORSELINE APPARENTLY WENT ON TO DESCRIBE LEAVING THE CAR TO SEE WHAT HAPPENED.
ONLY TO ENCOUNTER HENRY STEVENS, CARRYING A REVOLVER.
WHAT THE HELL ARE YOU DOING HERE?
THIS IS NONE OF YOUR AFFAIR!
STEVENS THEN FIRED HIS GUN INTO THE GROUND.
BUT NOW, ON THE STAND, THE MAN HAS SECOND THOUGHTS.
AFTER HEARING THE SHOTS, HE SAYS, HE AND THE LADY SIMPLY SPED AWAY FROM THE SCENE.

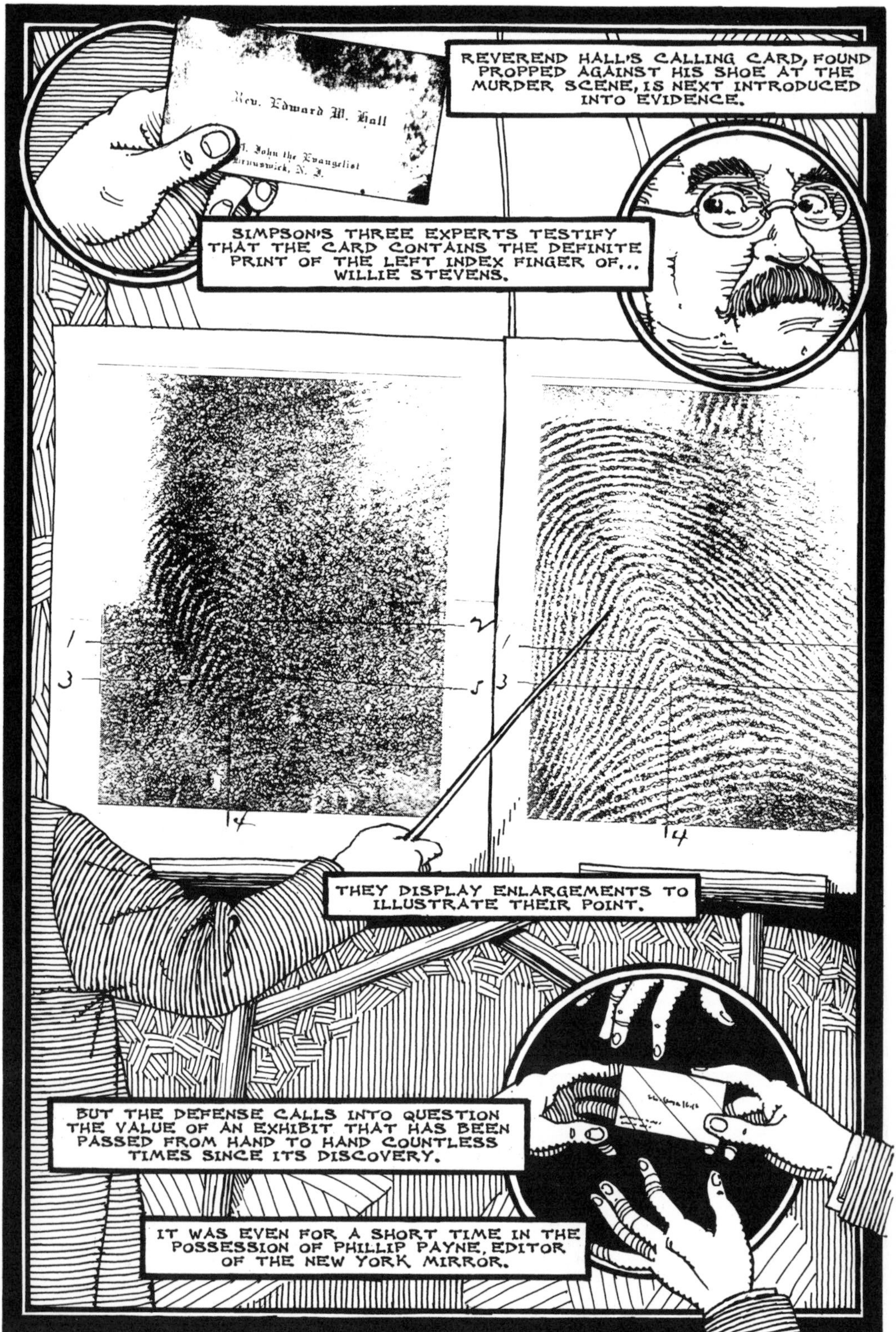

Rev. Edward W. Hall
REVEREND HALL'S CALLING CARD, FOUND PROPPED AGAINST HIS SHOE AT THE MURDER SCENE, IS NEXT INTRODUCED INTO EVIDENCE.
SIMPSON'S THREE EXPERTS TESTIFY THAT THE CARD CONTAINS THE DEFINITE PRINT OF THE LEFT INDEX FINGER OF... WILLIE STEVENS.
THEY DISPLAY ENLARGEMENTS TO ILLUSTRATE THEIR POINT.
BUT THE DEFENSE CALLS INTO QUESTION THE VALUE OF AN EXHIBIT THAT HAS BEEN PASSED FROM HAND TO HAND COUNTLESS TIMES SINCE ITS DISCOVERY.
IT WAS EVEN FOR A SHORT TIME IN THE POSSESSION OF PHILLIP PAYNE, EDITOR OF THE NEW YORK MIRROR.

DR. OTTO SCHULTZE, WHO CONDUCTED THE LATEST AUTOPSIES, INTRODUCES AN ANATOMICAL MODEL...

TO ILLUSTRATE THE PATHS OF THE BULLETS THROUGH THE SKULLS OF BOTH VICTIMS.

DURING THIS DEMONSTRATION, MRS. HALL AVERTS HER EYES AND IS SEEN TO RUMMAGE THROUGH HER POCKETBOOK.

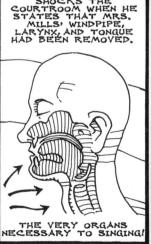

DR. SCHULTZE FURTHER SHOCKS THE COURTROOM WHEN HE STATES THAT MRS. MILLS' WINDPIPE, LARYNX, AND TONGUE HAD BEEN REMOVED.

THE VERY ORGANS NECESSARY TO SINGING!

THIS REVELATION BRINGS THE CRIME TO A LEVEL OF SAVAGERY NEVER BEFORE IMAGINED.

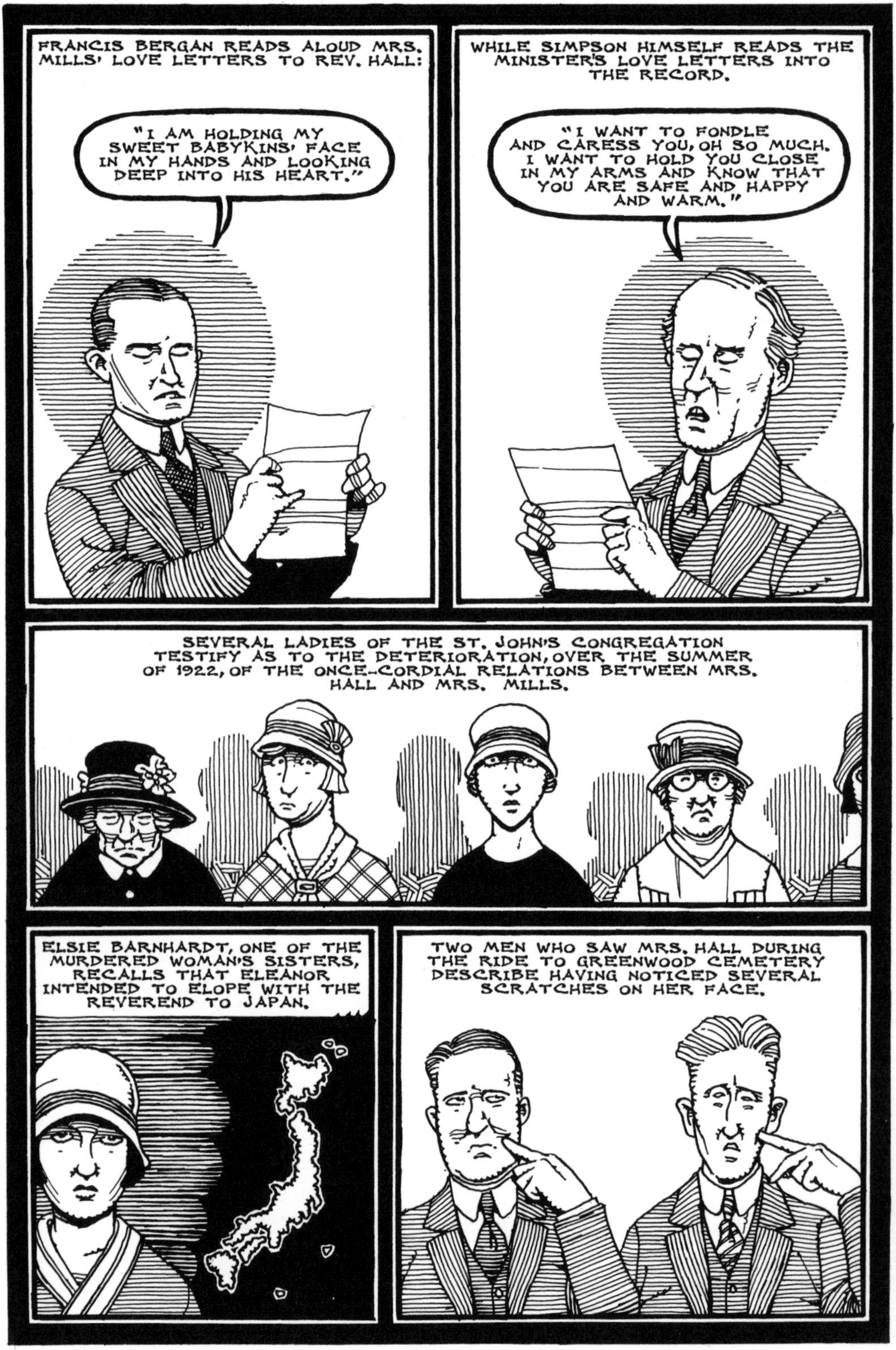
FRANCIS BERGAN READS ALOUD MRS. MILLS' LOVE LETTERS TO REV. HALL:
"I AM HOLDING MY SWEET BABYKINS' FACE IN MY HANDS AND LOOKING DEEP INTO HIS HEART."
WHILE SIMPSON HIMSELF READS THE MINISTER'S LOVE LETTERS INTO THE RECORD.
"I WANT TO FONDLE AND CARESS YOU, OH SO MUCH. I WANT TO HOLD YOU CLOSE IN MY ARMS AND KNOW THAT YOU ARE SAFE AND HAPPY AND WARM."
SEVERAL LADIES OF THE ST. JOHN'S CONGREGATION TESTIFY AS TO THE DETERIORATION, OVER THE SUMMER OF 1922, OF THE ONCE-CORDIAL RELATIONS BETWEEN MRS. HALL AND MRS. MILLS.
ELSIE BARNHARDT, ONE OF THE MURDERED WOMAN'S SISTERS, RECALLS THAT ELEANOR INTENDED TO ELOPE WITH THE REVEREND TO JAPAN.
TWO MEN WHO SAW MRS. HALL DURING THE RIDE TO GREENWOOD CEMETERY DESCRIBE HAVING NOTICED SEVERAL SCRATCHES ON HER FACE.

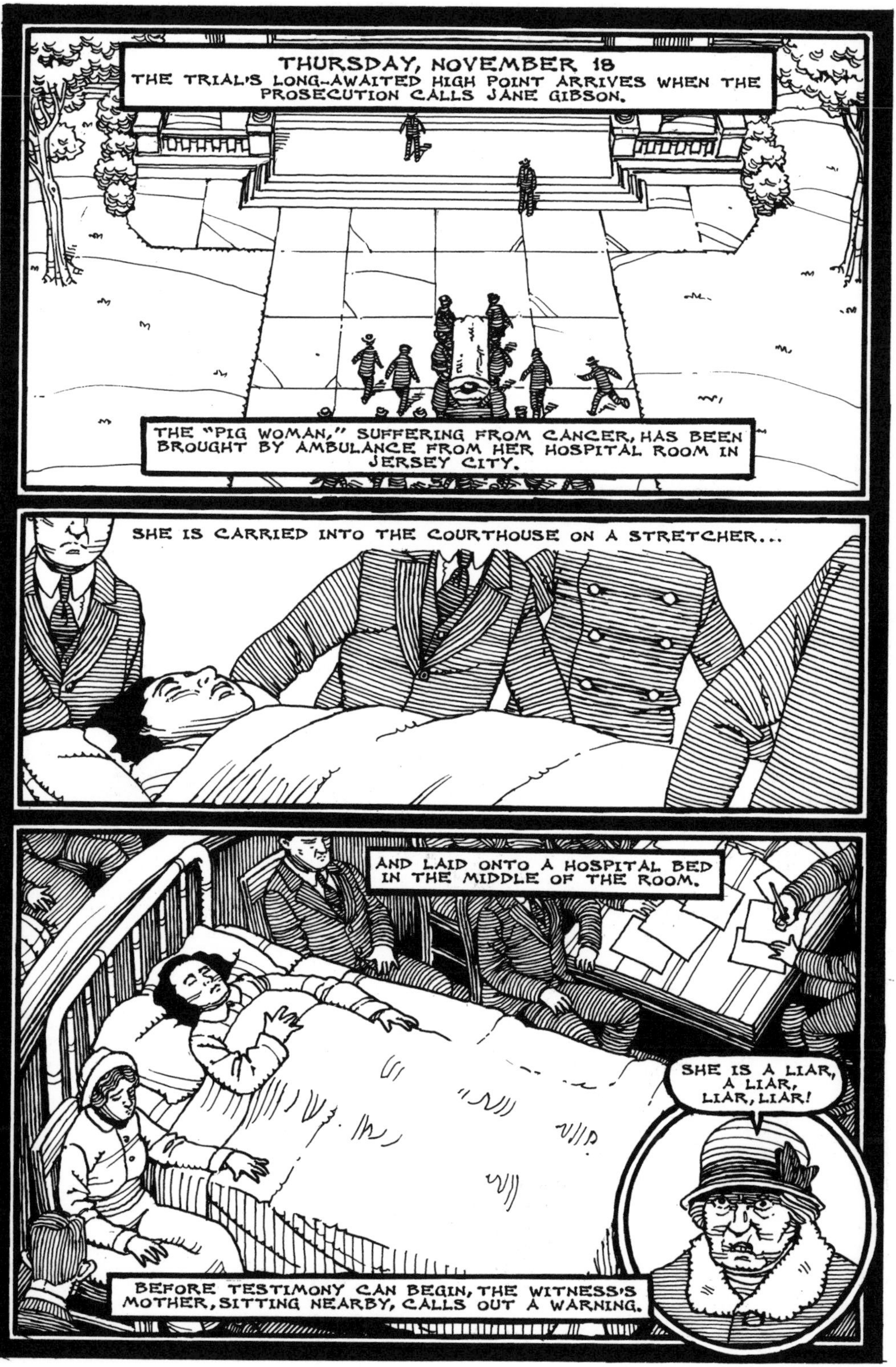
THURSDAY, NOVEMBER 18
THE TRIAL'S LONG-AWAITED HIGH POINT ARRIVES WHEN THE PROSECUTION CALLS JANE GIBSON.
THE "PIG WOMAN," SUFFERING FROM CANCER, HAS BEEN BROUGHT BY AMBULANCE FROM HER HOSPITAL ROOM IN JERSEY CITY.
SHE IS CARRIED INTO THE COURTHOUSE ON A STRETCHER...
AND LAID ONTO A HOSPITAL BED IN THE MIDDLE OF THE ROOM.
SHE IS A LIAR, A LIAR, LIAR, LIAR!
BEFORE TESTIMONY CAN BEGIN, THE WITNESS'S MOTHER, SITTING NEARBY, CALLS OUT A WARNING.

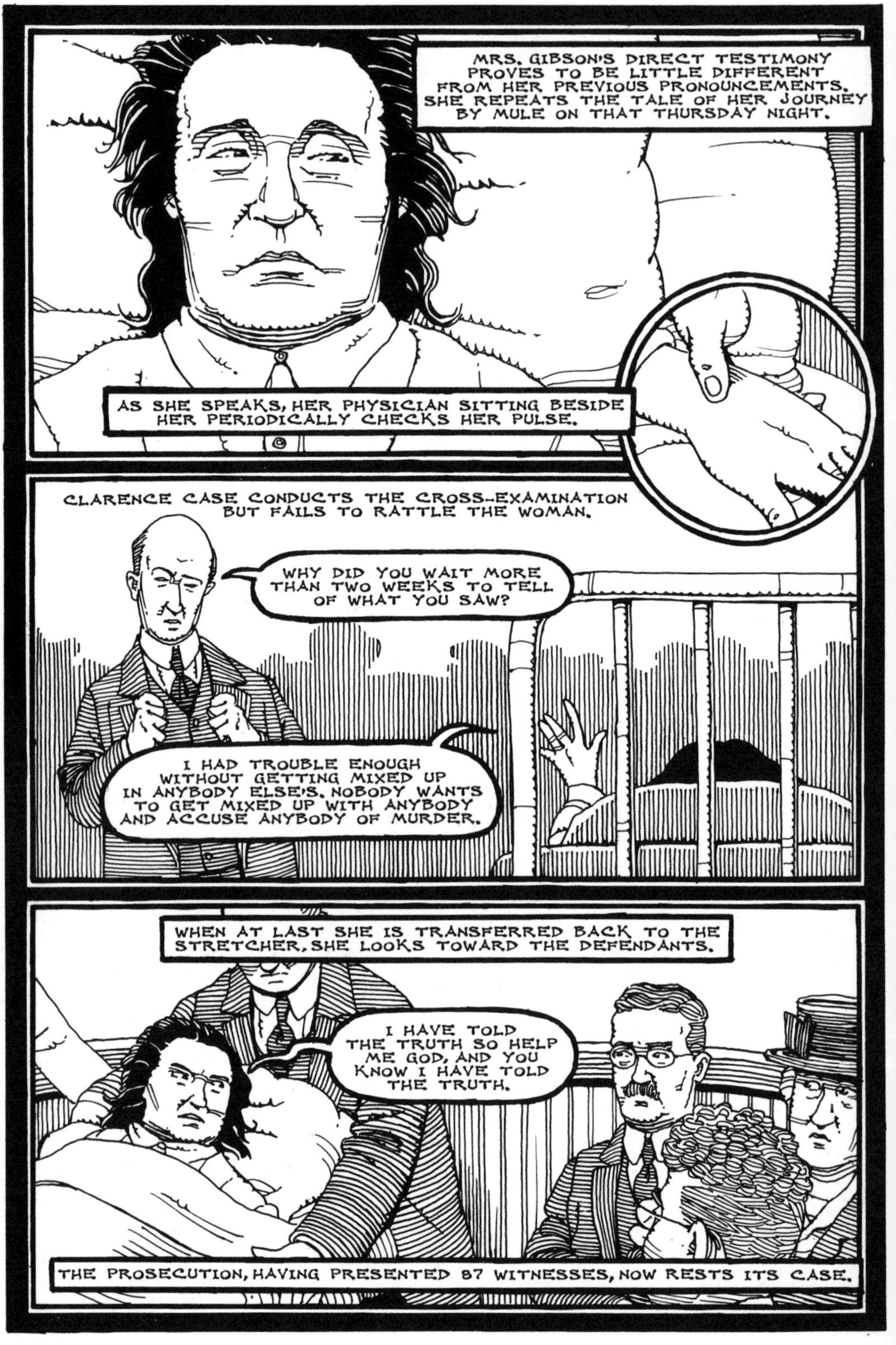
MRS. GIBSON'S DIRECT TESTIMONY PROVES TO BE LITTLE DIFFERENT FROM HER PREVIOUS PRONOUNCEMENTS. SHE REPEATS THE TALE OF HER JOURNEY BY MULE ON THAT THURSDAY NIGHT.
AS SHE SPEAKS, HER PHYSICIAN SITTING BESIDE HER PERIODICALLY CHECKS HER PULSE.
CLARENCE CASE CONDUCTS THE CROSS-EXAMINATION BUT FAILS TO RATTLE THE WOMAN.
WHY DID YOU WAIT MORE THAN TWO WEEKS TO TELL OF WHAT YOU SAW?
I HAD TROUBLE ENOUGH WITHOUT GETTING MIXED UP IN ANYBODY ELSE'S. NOBODY WANTS TO GET MIXED UP WITH ANYBODY AND ACCUSE ANYBODY OF MURDER.
WHEN AT LAST SHE IS TRANSFERRED BACK TO THE STRETCHER, SHE LOOKS TOWARD THE DEFENDANTS.
I HAVE TOLD THE TRUTH SO HELP ME GOD, AND YOU KNOW I HAVE TOLD THE TRUTH.
THE PROSECUTION, HAVING PRESENTED 87 WITNESSES, NOW RESTS ITS CASE.

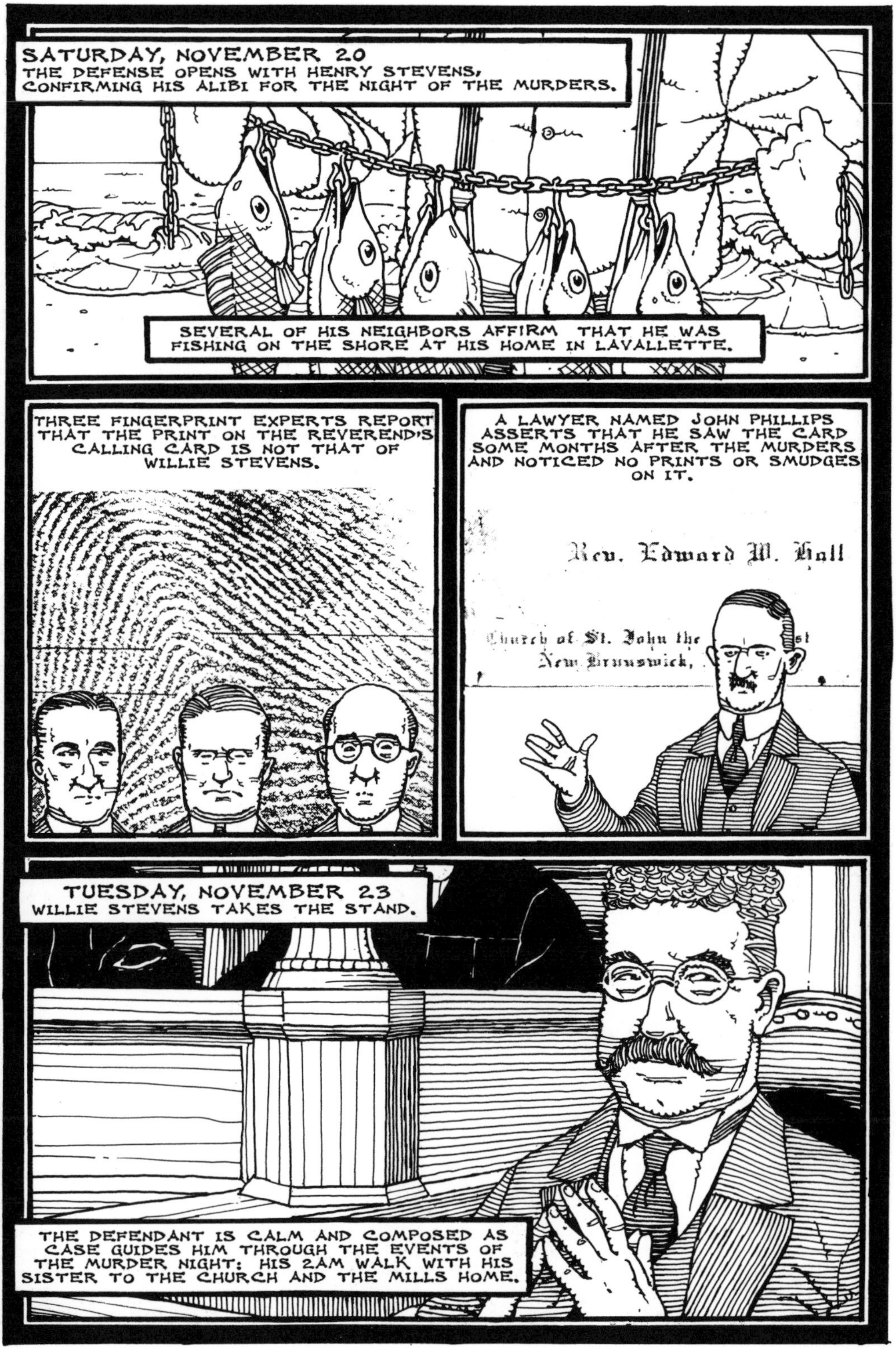
SATURDAY, NOVEMBER 20
THE DEFENSE OPENS WITH HENRY STEVENS, CONFIRMING HIS ALIBI FOR THE NIGHT OF THE MURDERS.
SEVERAL OF HIS NEIGHBORS AFFIRM THAT HE WAS FISHING ON THE SHORE AT HIS HOME IN LAVALLETTE.
THREE FINGERPRINT EXPERTS REPORT THAT THE PRINT ON THE REVEREND'S CALLING CARD IS NOT THAT OF WILLIE STEVENS.
A LAWYER NAMED JOHN PHILLIPS ASSERTS THAT HE SAW THE CARD SOME MONTHS AFTER THE MURDERS AND NOTICED NO PRINTS OR SMUDGES ON IT.
Rev. Edward W. Hall
Church of St. John the
New Brunswick,
TUESDAY, NOVEMBER 23
WILLIE STEVENS TAKES THE STAND.
THE DEFENDANT IS CALM AND COMPOSED AS CASE GUIDES HIM THROUGH THE EVENTS OF THE MURDER NIGHT: HIS 2AM WALK WITH HIS SISTER TO THE CHURCH AND THE MILLS HOME.

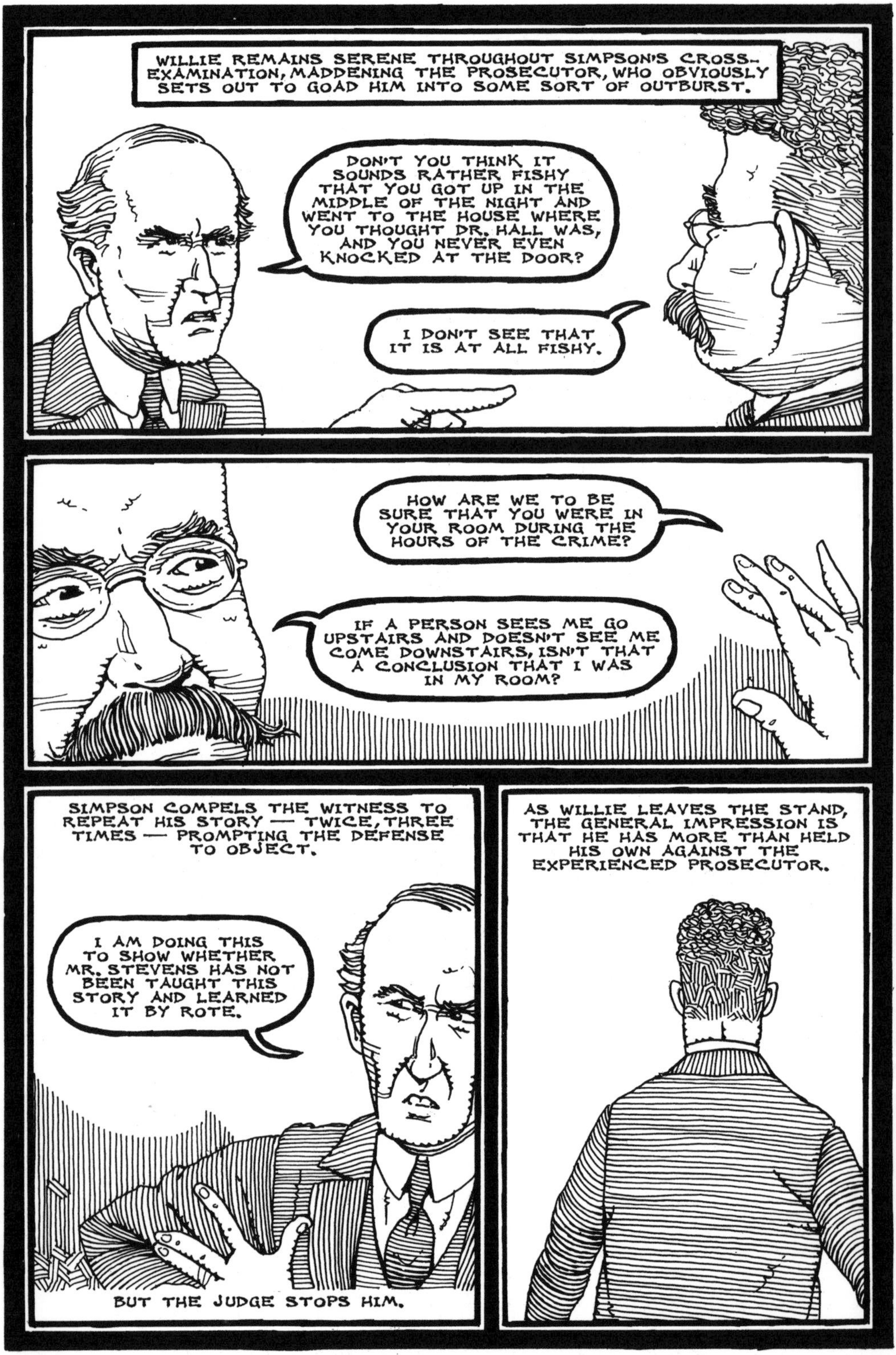
WILLIE REMAINS SERENE THROUGHOUT SIMPSON'S CROSS-EXAMINATION, MADDENING THE PROSECUTOR, WHO OBVIOUSLY SETS OUT TO GOAD HIM INTO SOME SORT OF OUTBURST.
DON'T YOU THINK IT SOUNDS RATHER FISHY THAT YOU GOT UP IN THE MIDDLE OF THE NIGHT AND WENT TO THE HOUSE WHERE YOU THOUGHT DR. HALL WAS, AND YOU NEVER EVEN KNOCKED AT THE DOOR?
I DON'T SEE THAT IT IS AT ALL FISHY.
HOW ARE WE TO BE SURE THAT YOU WERE IN YOUR ROOM DURING THE HOURS OF THE CRIME?
IF A PERSON SEES ME GO UPSTAIRS AND DOESN'T SEE ME COME DOWNSTAIRS, ISN'T THAT A CONCLUSION THAT I WAS IN MY ROOM?
SIMPSON COMPELS THE WITNESS TO REPEAT HIS STORY — TWICE, THREE TIMES — PROMPTING THE DEFENSE TO OBJECT.
I AM DOING THIS TO SHOW WHETHER MR. STEVENS HAS NOT BEEN TAUGHT THIS STORY AND LEARNED IT BY ROTE.
BUT THE JUDGE STOPS HIM.
AS WILLIE LEAVES THE STAND, THE GENERAL IMPRESSION IS THAT HE HAS MORE THAN HELD HIS OWN AGAINST THE EXPERIENCED PROSECUTOR.

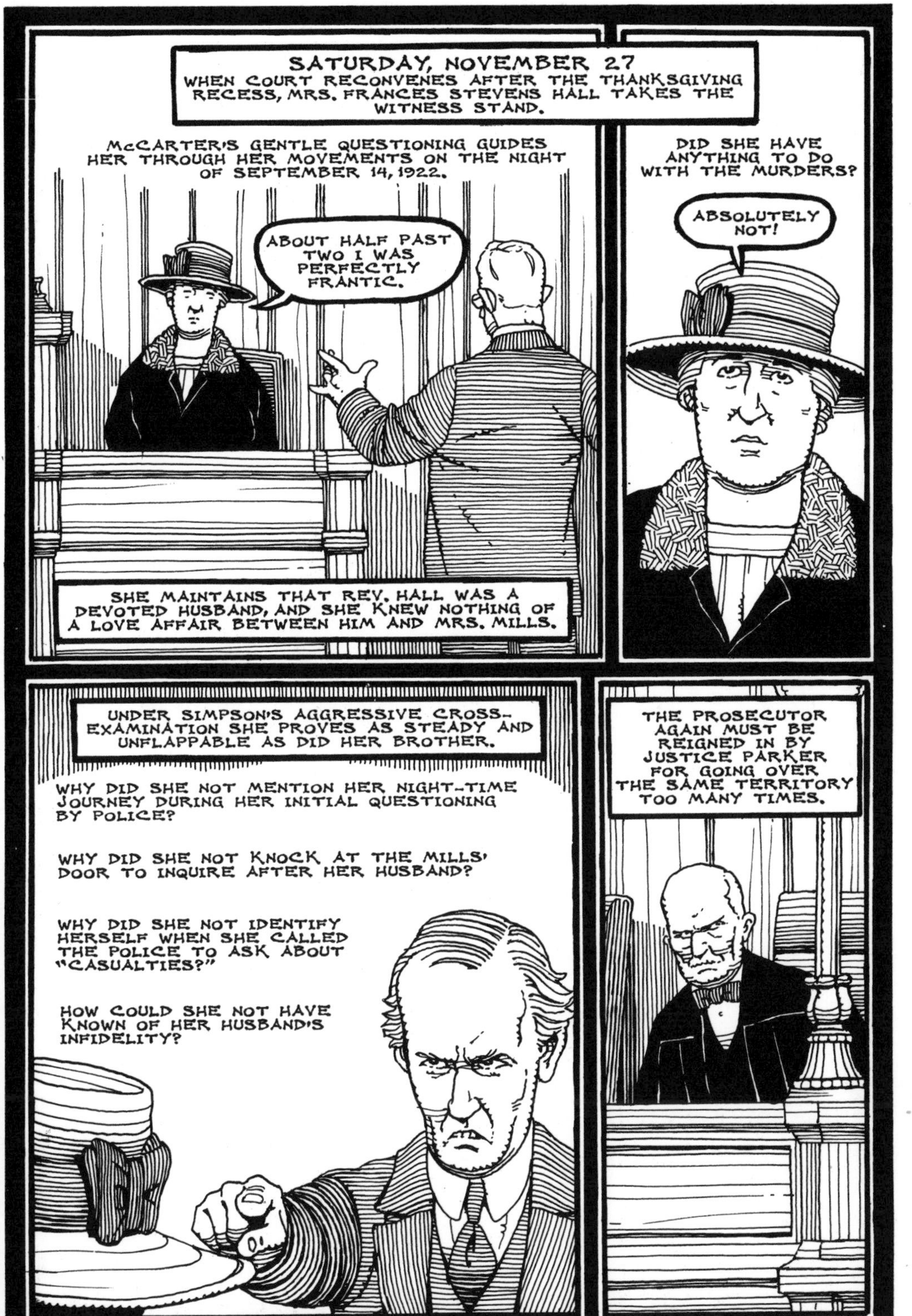
SATURDAY, NOVEMBER 27
WHEN COURT RECONVENES AFTER THE THANKSGIVING RECESS, MRS. FRANCES STEVENS HALL TAKES THE WITNESS STAND.
McCARTER'S GENTLE QUESTIONING GUIDES HER THROUGH HER MOVEMENTS ON THE NIGHT OF SEPTEMBER 14, 1922.
ABOUT HALF PAST TWO I WAS PERFECTLY FRANTIC.
SHE MAINTAINS THAT REV. HALL WAS A DEVOTED HUSBAND, AND SHE KNEW NOTHING OF A LOVE AFFAIR BETWEEN HIM AND MRS. MILLS.
DID SHE HAVE ANYTHING TO DO WITH THE MURDERS?
ABSOLUTELY NOT!
UNDER SIMPSON'S AGGRESSIVE CROSS-EXAMINATION SHE PROVES AS STEADY AND UNFLAPPABLE AS DID HER BROTHER.
WHY DID SHE NOT MENTION HER NIGHT-TIME JOURNEY DURING HER INITIAL QUESTIONING BY POLICE?
WHY DID SHE NOT KNOCK AT THE MILLS' DOOR TO INQUIRE AFTER HER HUSBAND?
WHY DID SHE NOT IDENTIFY HERSELF WHEN SHE CALLED THE POLICE TO ASK ABOUT "CASUALTIES?"
HOW COULD SHE NOT HAVE KNOWN OF HER HUSBAND'S INFIDELITY?
THE PROSECUTOR AGAIN MUST BE REIGNED IN BY JUSTICE PARKER FOR GOING OVER THE SAME TERRITORY TOO MANY TIMES.

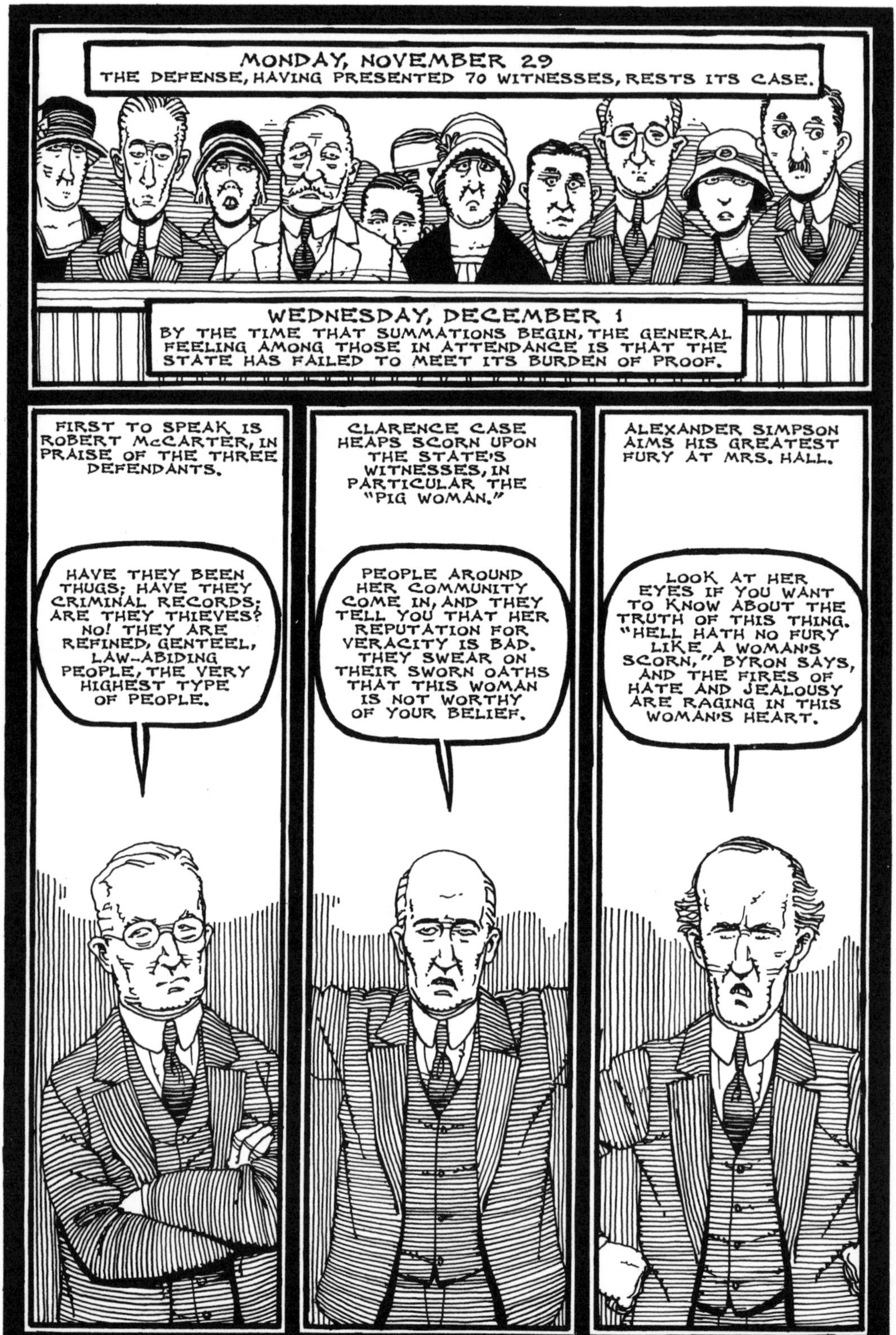
MONDAY, NOVEMBER 29
THE DEFENSE, HAVING PRESENTED 70 WITNESSES, RESTS ITS CASE.
WEDNESDAY, DECEMBER 1
BY THE TIME THAT SUMMATIONS BEGIN, THE GENERAL FEELING AMONG THOSE IN ATTENDANCE IS THAT THE STATE HAS FAILED TO MEET ITS BURDEN OF PROOF.
FIRST TO SPEAK IS ROBERT McCARTER, IN PRAISE OF THE THREE DEFENDANTS.
HAVE THEY BEEN THUGS; HAVE THEY CRIMINAL RECORDS; ARE THEY THIEVES? NO! THEY ARE REFINED, GENTEEL, LAW-ABIDING PEOPLE, THE VERY HIGHEST TYPE OF PEOPLE.
CLARENCE CASE HEAPS SCORN UPON THE STATE'S WITNESSES, IN PARTICULAR THE "PIG WOMAN."
PEOPLE AROUND HER COMMUNITY COME IN, AND THEY TELL YOU THAT HER REPUTATION FOR VERACITY IS BAD. THEY SWEAR ON THEIR SWORN OATHS THAT THIS WOMAN IS NOT WORTHY OF YOUR BELIEF.
ALEXANDER SIMPSON AIMS HIS GREATEST FURY AT MRS. HALL.
LOOK AT HER EYES IF YOU WANT TO KNOW ABOUT THE TRUTH OF THIS THING. "HELL HATH NO FURY LIKE A WOMAN'S SCORN," BYRON SAYS, AND THE FIRES OF HATE AND JEALOUSY ARE RAGING IN THIS WOMAN'S HEART.

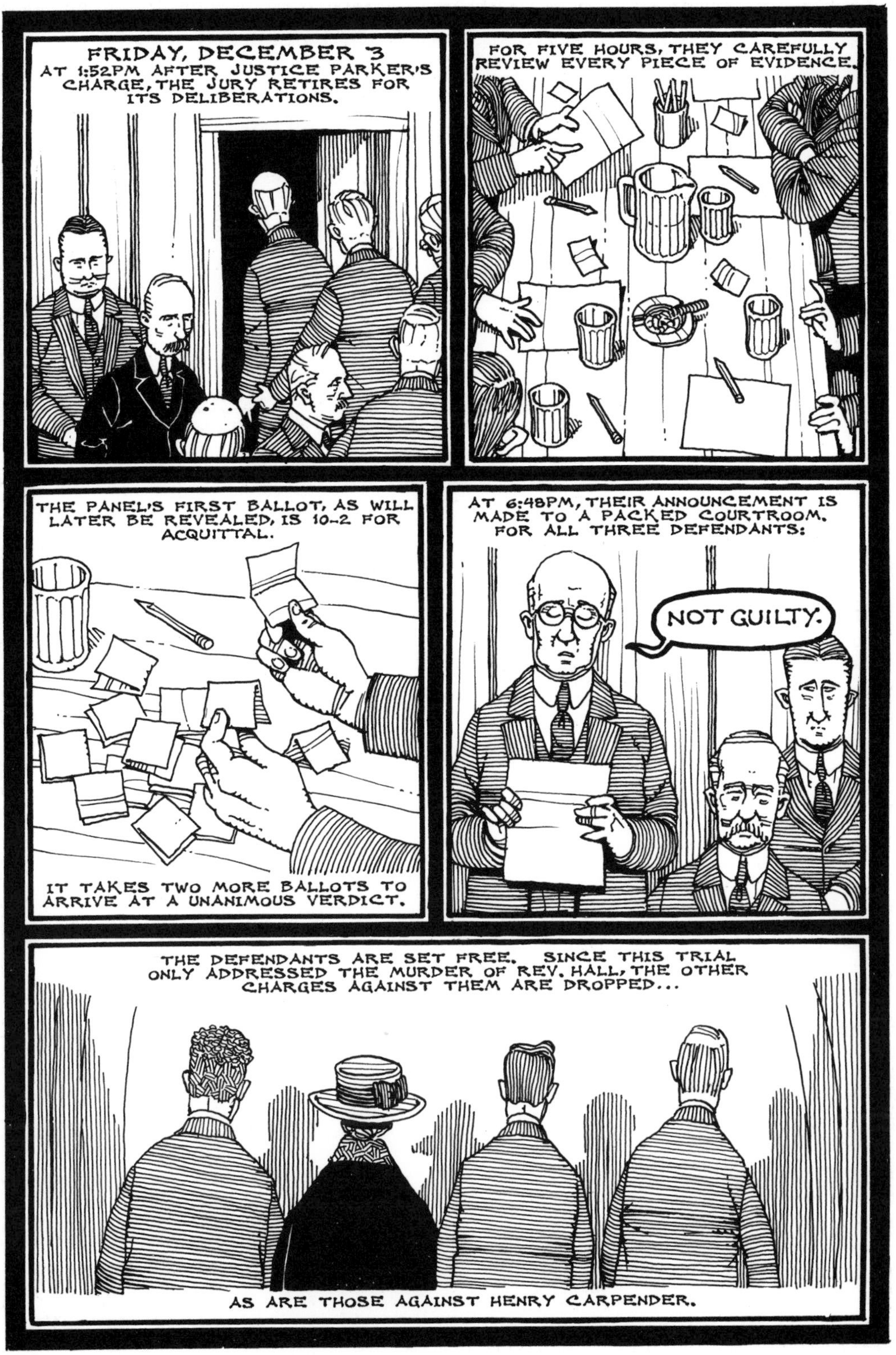
FRIDAY, DECEMBER 3
AT 1:52PM AFTER JUSTICE PARKER'S CHARGE, THE JURY RETIRES FOR ITS DELIBERATIONS.
FOR FIVE HOURS, THEY CAREFULLY REVIEW EVERY PIECE OF EVIDENCE.
THE PANEL'S FIRST BALLOT, AS WILL LATER BE REVEALED, IS 10-2 FOR ACQUITTAL.
IT TAKES TWO MORE BALLOTS TO ARRIVE AT A UNANIMOUS VERDICT.
AT 6:48PM, THEIR ANNOUNCEMENT IS MADE TO A PACKED COURTROOM. FOR ALL THREE DEFENDANTS:
NOT GUILTY.
THE DEFENDANTS ARE SET FREE. SINCE THIS TRIAL ONLY ADDRESSED THE MURDER OF REV. HALL, THE OTHER CHARGES AGAINST THEM ARE DROPPED...
AS ARE THOSE AGAINST HENRY CARPENDER.

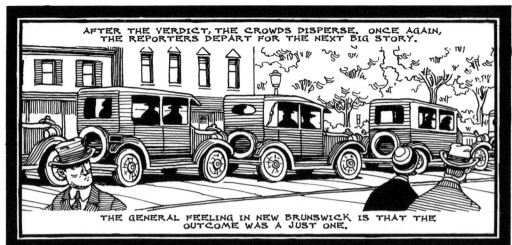

AFTER THE VERDICT, THE CROWDS DISPERSE. ONCE AGAIN, THE REPORTERS DEPART FOR THE NEXT BIG STORY.

THE GENERAL FEELING IN NEW BRUNSWICK IS THAT THE OUTCOME WAS A JUST ONE.

BUT MANY REMAIN UNSATISFIED, CHIEF AMONG THEM CHARLOTTE MILLS AND HER FATHER.

MONEY CAN BUY ANYTHING.

MRS. HALL AND HER BROTHER WILLIE RETURN TO THEIR QUIET LIVES ON NICHOL AVENUE...

NEVER AGAIN TO SPEAK PUBLICLY THEIR ORDEAL.

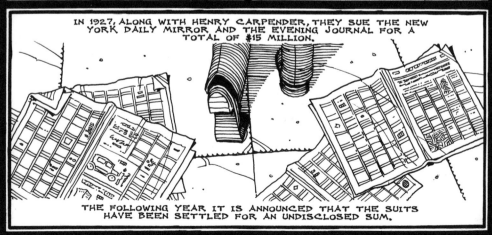

IN 1927, ALONG WITH HENRY CARPENDER, THEY SUE THE NEW YORK DAILY MIRROR AND THE EVENING JOURNAL FOR A TOTAL OF $15 MILLION.

THE FOLLOWING YEAR IT IS ANNOUNCED THAT THE SUITS HAVE BEEN SETTLED FOR AN UNDISCLOSED SUM.

PART VI

WHO DID IT?

THE HALL–MILLS CASE REMAINS AN OPEN ONE ON THE
BOOKS OF SOMERSET COUNTY.

OVER THE YEARS THERE HAS BEEN NO WANT OF
SPECULATION AS TO WHAT ACTUALLY HAPPENED ON LOVERS'
LANE THAT THURSDAY NIGHT IN 1922.

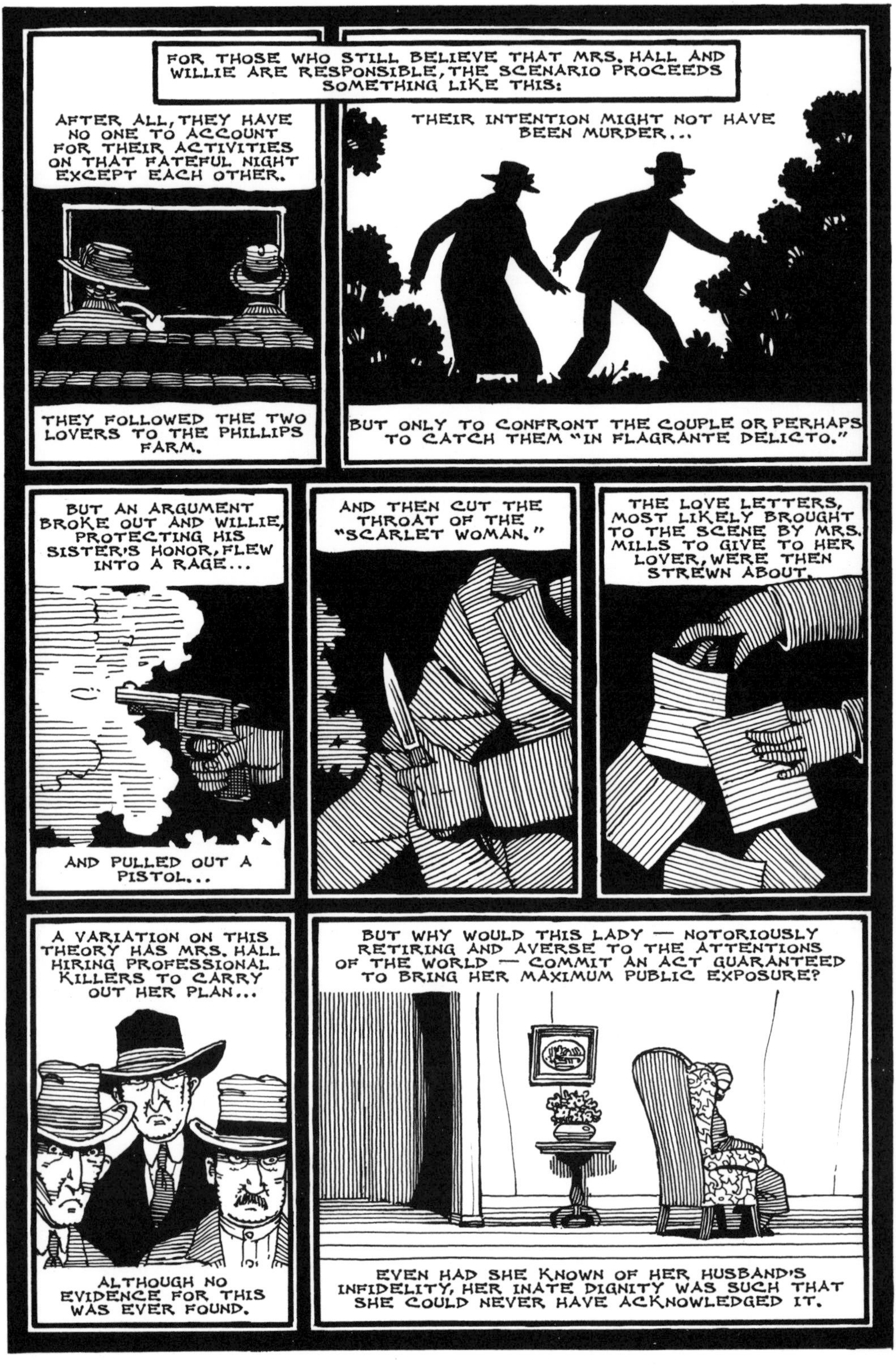

FOR THOSE WHO STILL BELIEVE THAT MRS. HALL AND WILLIE ARE RESPONSIBLE, THE SCENARIO PROCEEDS SOMETHING LIKE THIS:
AFTER ALL, THEY HAVE NO ONE TO ACCOUNT FOR THEIR ACTIVITIES ON THAT FATEFUL NIGHT EXCEPT EACH OTHER.
THEY FOLLOWED THE TWO LOVERS TO THE PHILLIPS FARM.
THEIR INTENTION MIGHT NOT HAVE BEEN MURDER...
BUT ONLY TO CONFRONT THE COUPLE OR PERHAPS TO CATCH THEM "IN FLAGRANTE DELICTO."
BUT AN ARGUMENT BROKE OUT AND WILLIE, PROTECTING HIS SISTER'S HONOR, FLEW INTO A RAGE...
AND PULLED OUT A PISTOL...
AND THEN CUT THE THROAT OF THE "SCARLET WOMAN."
THE LOVE LETTERS, MOST LIKELY BROUGHT TO THE SCENE BY MRS. MILLS TO GIVE TO HER LOVER, WERE THEN STREWN ABOUT.
A VARIATION ON THIS THEORY HAS MRS. HALL HIRING PROFESSIONAL KILLERS TO CARRY OUT HER PLAN...
ALTHOUGH NO EVIDENCE FOR THIS WAS EVER FOUND.
BUT WHY WOULD THIS LADY — NOTORIOUSLY RETIRING AND AVERSE TO THE ATTENTIONS OF THE WORLD — COMMIT AN ACT GUARANTEED TO BRING HER MAXIMUM PUBLIC EXPOSURE?
EVEN HAD SHE KNOWN OF HER HUSBAND'S INFIDELITY, HER INATE DIGNITY WAS SUCH THAT SHE COULD NEVER HAVE ACKNOWLEDGED IT.

ANOTHER THEORY NAMES JAMES MILLS, WHO, LIKE MRS. HALL, HAD THE STRONGEST MOTIVE FOR THE CRIME.

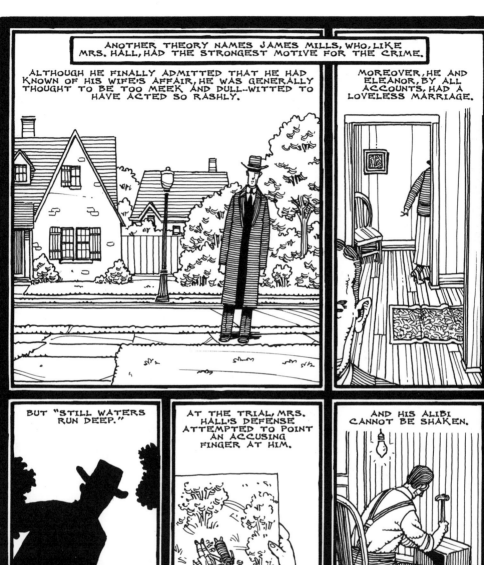

ALTHOUGH HE FINALLY ADMITTED THAT HE HAD KNOWN OF HIS WIFE'S AFFAIR, HE WAS GENERALLY THOUGHT TO BE TOO MEEK AND DULL-WITTED TO HAVE ACTED SO RASHLY.

MOREOVER, HE AND ELEANOR, BY ALL ACCOUNTS, HAD A LOVELESS MARRIAGE.

BUT "STILL WATERS RUN DEEP."

AND THIS QUIET MAN COULD HAVE NURSED A VIOLENT PASSION THAT NOBODY ELSE COULD GUESS AT.

AT THE TRIAL, MRS. HALL'S DEFENSE ATTEMPTED TO POINT AN ACCUSING FINGER AT HIM.

ALTHOUGH, AS WITH THE WIDOW, NO DIRECT EVIDENCE PLACES HIM AT THE SCENE.

AND HIS ALIBI CANNOT BE SHAKEN.

AMPLE TESTIMONY PLACED HIM AT HOME WORKING ON WINDOW BOXES DURING THE CRITICAL HOURS.

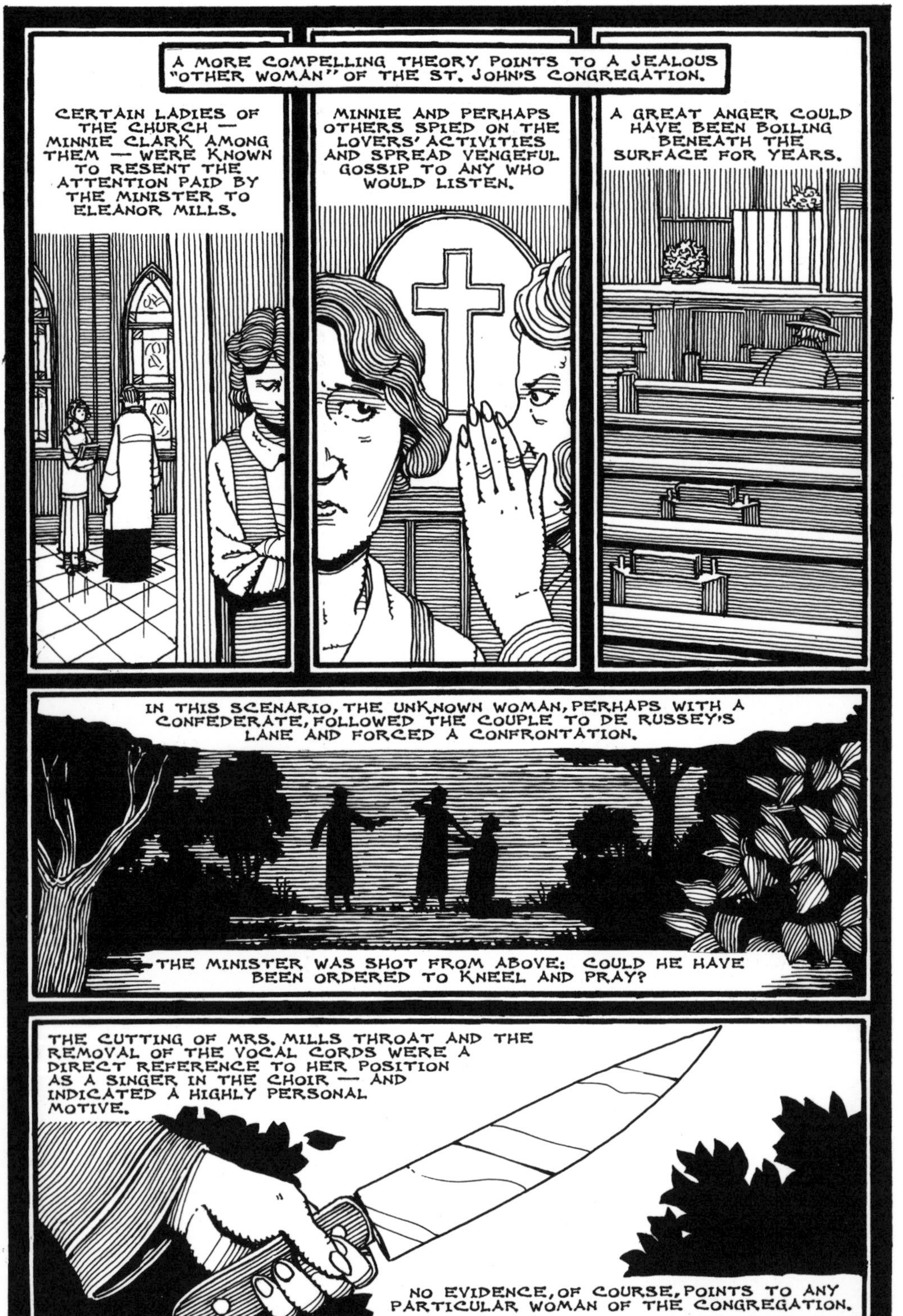
A MORE COMPELLING THEORY POINTS TO A JEALOUS "OTHER WOMAN" OF THE ST. JOHN'S CONGREGATION.
CERTAIN LADIES OF THE CHURCH — MINNIE CLARK AMONG THEM — WERE KNOWN TO RESENT THE ATTENTION PAID BY THE MINISTER TO ELEANOR MILLS.
MINNIE AND PERHAPS OTHERS SPIED ON THE LOVERS' ACTIVITIES AND SPREAD VENGEFUL GOSSIP TO ANY WHO WOULD LISTEN.
A GREAT ANGER COULD HAVE BEEN BOILING BENEATH THE SURFACE FOR YEARS.
IN THIS SCENARIO, THE UNKNOWN WOMAN, PERHAPS WITH A CONFEDERATE, FOLLOWED THE COUPLE TO DE RUSSEY'S LANE AND FORCED A CONFRONTATION.
THE MINISTER WAS SHOT FROM ABOVE: COULD HE HAVE BEEN ORDERED TO KNEEL AND PRAY?
THE CUTTING OF MRS. MILLS THROAT AND THE REMOVAL OF THE VOCAL CORDS WERE A DIRECT REFERENCE TO HER POSITION AS A SINGER IN THE CHOIR — AND INDICATED A HIGHLY PERSONAL MOTIVE.
NO EVIDENCE, OF COURSE, POINTS TO ANY PARTICULAR WOMAN OF THE CONGREGATION.

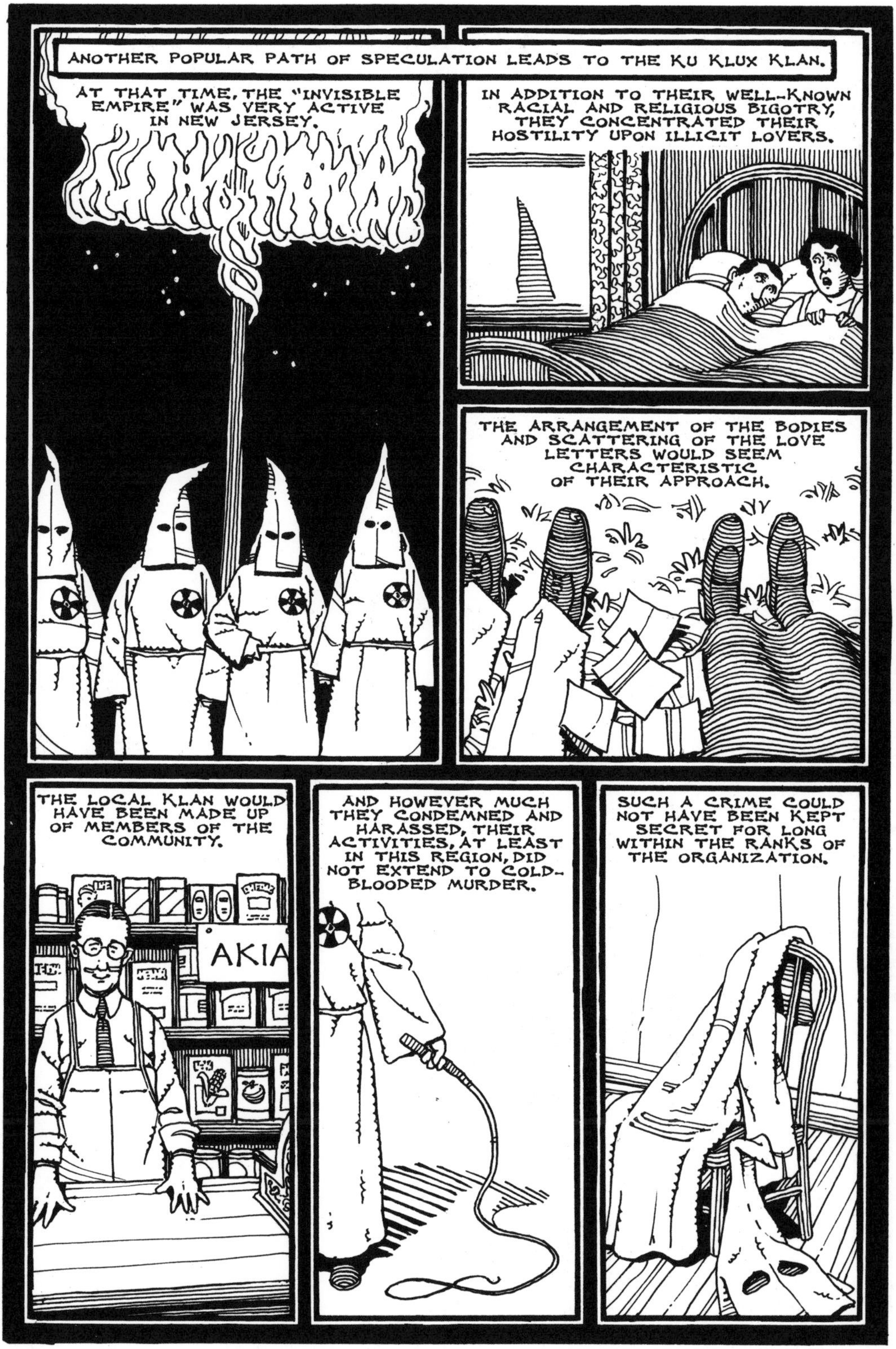
ANOTHER POPULAR PATH OF SPECULATION LEADS TO THE KU KLUX KLAN.
AT THAT TIME, THE "INVISIBLE EMPIRE" WAS VERY ACTIVE IN NEW JERSEY.
IN ADDITION TO THEIR WELL-KNOWN RACIAL AND RELIGIOUS BIGOTRY, THEY CONCENTRATED THEIR HOSTILITY UPON ILLICIT LOVERS.
THE ARRANGEMENT OF THE BODIES AND SCATTERING OF THE LOVE LETTERS WOULD SEEM CHARACTERISTIC OF THEIR APPROACH.
THE LOCAL KLAN WOULD HAVE BEEN MADE UP OF MEMBERS OF THE COMMUNITY.
AKIA
AND HOWEVER MUCH THEY CONDEMNED AND HARASSED, THEIR ACTIVITIES, AT LEAST IN THIS REGION, DID NOT EXTEND TO COLD-BLOODED MURDER.
SUCH A CRIME COULD NOT HAVE BEEN KEPT SECRET FOR LONG WITHIN THE RANKS OF THE ORGANIZATION.

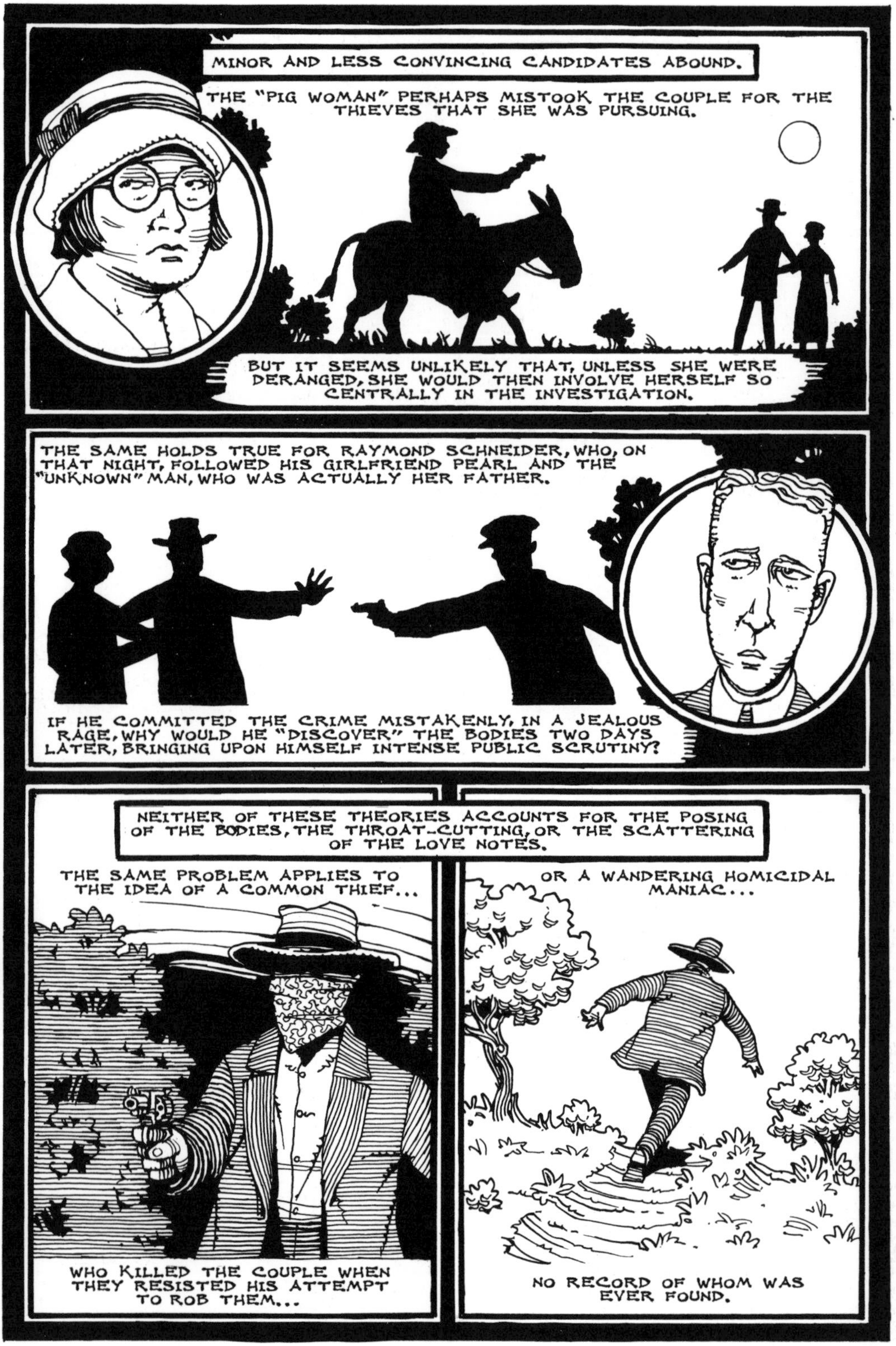
MINOR AND LESS CONVINCING CANDIDATES ABOUND.
THE "PIG WOMAN" PERHAPS MISTOOK THE COUPLE FOR THE THIEVES THAT SHE WAS PURSUING.
BUT IT SEEMS UNLIKELY THAT, UNLESS SHE WERE DERANGED, SHE WOULD THEN INVOLVE HERSELF SO CENTRALLY IN THE INVESTIGATION.
THE SAME HOLDS TRUE FOR RAYMOND SCHNEIDER, WHO, ON THAT NIGHT, FOLLOWED HIS GIRLFRIEND PEARL AND THE "UNKNOWN" MAN, WHO WAS ACTUALLY HER FATHER.
IF HE COMMITTED THE CRIME MISTAKENLY, IN A JEALOUS RAGE, WHY WOULD HE "DISCOVER" THE BODIES TWO DAYS LATER, BRINGING UPON HIMSELF INTENSE PUBLIC SCRUTINY?
NEITHER OF THESE THEORIES ACCOUNTS FOR THE POSING OF THE BODIES, THE THROAT-CUTTING, OR THE SCATTERING OF THE LOVE NOTES.
THE SAME PROBLEM APPLIES TO THE IDEA OF A COMMON THIEF...
WHO KILLED THE COUPLE WHEN THEY RESISTED HIS ATTEMPT TO ROB THEM...
OR A WANDERING HOMICIDAL MANIAC...
NO RECORD OF WHOM WAS EVER FOUND.

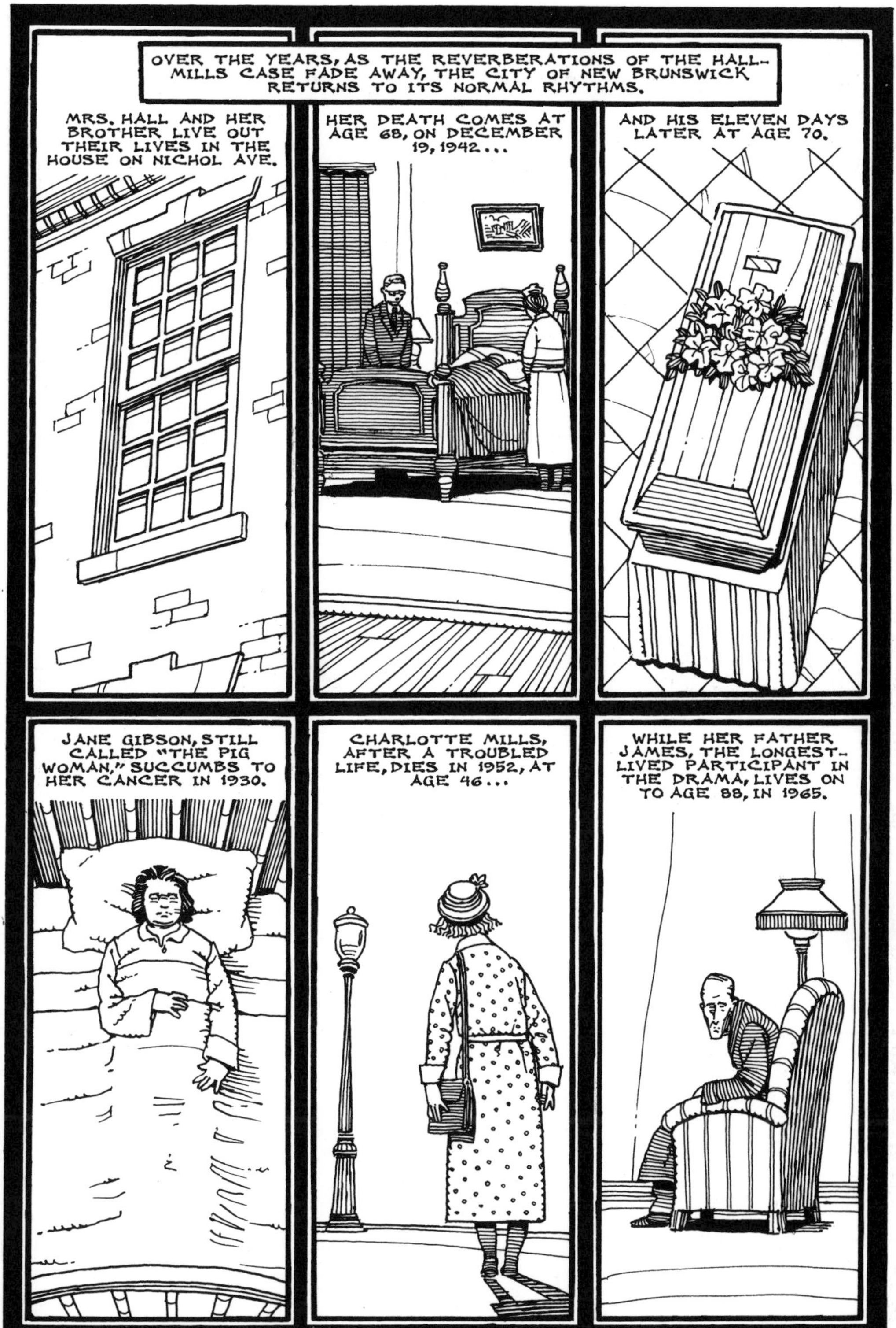
OVER THE YEARS, AS THE REVERBERATIONS OF THE HALL-MILLS CASE FADE AWAY, THE CITY OF NEW BRUNSWICK RETURNS TO ITS NORMAL RHYTHMS.
MRS. HALL AND HER BROTHER LIVE OUT THEIR LIVES IN THE HOUSE ON NICHOL AVE.
HER DEATH COMES AT AGE 68, ON DECEMBER 19, 1942...
AND HIS ELEVEN DAYS LATER AT AGE 70.
JANE GIBSON, STILL CALLED "THE PIG WOMAN," SUCCUMBS TO HER CANCER IN 1930.
CHARLOTTE MILLS, AFTER A TROUBLED LIFE, DIES IN 1952, AT AGE 46...
WHILE HER FATHER JAMES, THE LONGEST-LIVED PARTICIPANT IN THE DRAMA, LIVES ON TO AGE 88, IN 1965.

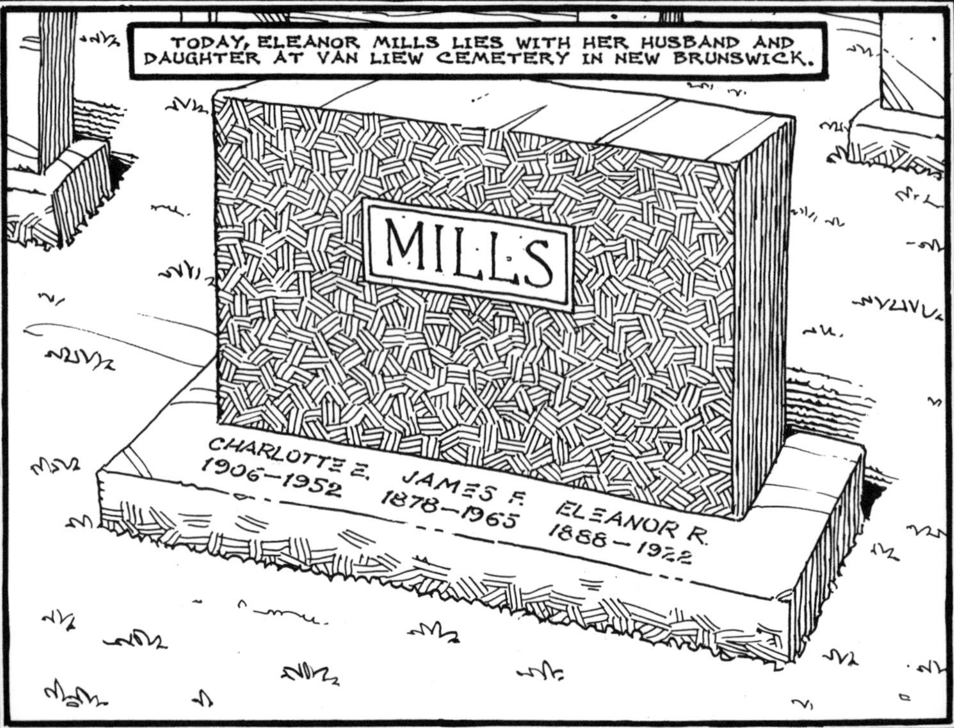
TODAY, ELEANOR MILLS LIES WITH HER HUSBAND AND DAUGHTER AT VAN LIEW CEMETERY IN NEW BRUNSWICK.
MILLS
CHARLOTTE E. 1906–1952
JAMES F. 1878–1965
ELEANOR R. 1888–1922

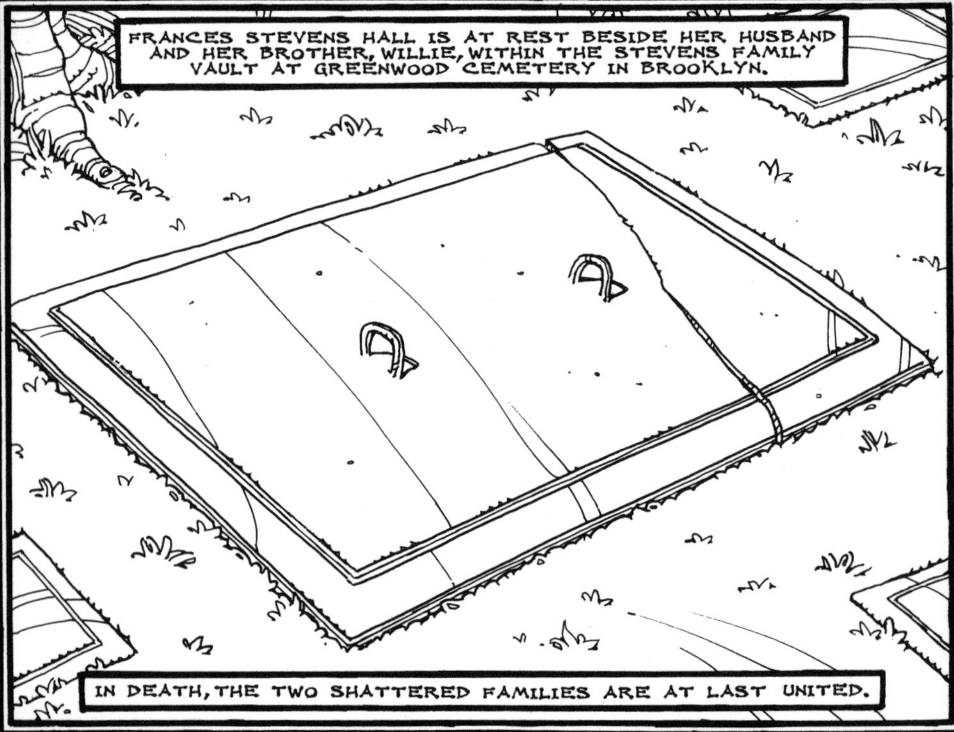
FRANCES STEVENS HALL IS AT REST BESIDE HER HUSBAND AND HER BROTHER, WILLIE, WITHIN THE STEVENS FAMILY VAULT AT GREENWOOD CEMETERY IN BROOKLYN.
IN DEATH, THE TWO SHATTERED FAMILIES ARE AT LAST UNITED.